TRIANGLE
The first DS Jackson thriller

Jonathan Cotty

TRIANGLE

Jonathan Cotty

Triangle © Jonathan Cotty

First Edition

Published Worldwide 2014

Copyright 2014 © Jonathan Cotty

ISBN: 1502345293

ISBN-13: 978-1502345295

To my fiancé, Chloe Hirst

Chapter 1

The three tower blocks comprising the northeast sector of Brook Hill estate stick out of the landscape like broken fingers. Solid and immovable, the tenements were hastily erected in the 1960s and are amongst the ugliest buildings in southern England. For years, the blocks have been awaiting demolition in line with the council's regeneration programme, but despite numerous proposals they remain in place, grimly awaiting their inevitable destruction. A few residents remain in situ, but the flats are now mostly empty and boarded up; the only visible sign of life on many floors is the fresh graffiti sprayed over the plywood panels. Shaded areas of the blocks remain permanently wet, patches of slimy, green algae clinging to the exterior and betraying the damp problems that have haunted the sink estate since its initial construction.

Parked up on a parallel street in an unmarked, blue, Vauxhall Astra, Detective Sergeant Raymond Jackson was underneath the easternmost block, Saffron Court. He listened to the intermittent shouting that fed down from the heights above as he munched on a chicken and sweetcorn sandwich. Occasionally a door or window opened and the row was briefly audible: a man yelling, a teenager swearing, a woman remonstrating and young children crying, before a faint slamming sound was immediately followed by more muffled shouting.

It was now mid-August and it had been baking hot for weeks. Through what remained of the wooden fence panelling to his left, Ray noticed a metal sign on the side of the tower block. The dark green paint was flaking and there was evidence it had been used for target practice at some point. A series of holes punctured the metal, unmistakably the type made by some kind of air gun. Despite the damage, the sign was still quite legible. 'NO BALL GAMES'. It looked ancient, infixed into the brickwork above the brown, parched turf, a silent testament to the children that had once played here.

'How many people still live here then, guv?'

His reverie broken, Ray glanced over at his colleague in the passenger seat and frowned. Jason Stephenson had only very recently joined CID as a Detective Constable. He was slim, young and ambitious, with spiky blonde hair and a narrow, pinched face.

'Not many,' Ray replied. He took another bite from his sandwich and washed it down with a swig of coke. 'Most…'

Without warning, Ray starting choking in spectacular fashion. Coke erupted from his mouth and nose whilst pieces of sweetcorn flew out in all directions. Aghast, Jason withdrew swiftly from his superior, a look of unmasked disgust on his face. He pressed himself back against the passenger door to avoid being sprayed, as bits of half-chewed chicken were projected back into the vehicle. Jason swiftly recovered himself, adopting a look of mock concern as he turned to his superior officer whilst Ray, still coughing and unable to speak, waved him away irritably with his right hand. Having opened his mouth to say something, Jason wisely closed it again and remained silent. He made a point of turning away from Ray to adjust his seatbelt, which had tightened round his body and neck like a boa constrictor following his initial reaction.

'Sorry about that,' said Ray, his breath still coming in gasps.

'You all right, guv?'

Ray cleared his throat. 'Yup.' There was slightly awkward pause, before Ray continued. 'It's mainly used by the homeless now, some of the flats have been used for vice from time to time. We closed a drug den down here a few years back, an op I was involved in. We only ever nailed the one guy though, selling heroin and giving punters a place to use.' Ray finished his sandwich with a single bite before he spoke again. 'He was actually not a bad bloke in many ways to be honest, he used to get clean needles from the methadone clinic down Bore Street and the stuff we found was pretty clean.'

'Clean?'

'Yeah, clean. As in it wasn't cut with anything too harmful, like quinine, or broken glass.'

'Oh, I see. A dealer who cares.'

Ray shrugged. 'It was a complicated story. He battled with addiction all his life and it also claimed the life of one of his nieces.

Not the heroin itself in the end, but due to her sharing a needle. He didn't deal to just anyone either.' Ray sighed. 'I'm not defending him, but life is not just black and white, not always anyway. I think in his own mind he actually thought he was helping. He also volunteered down at the methadone clinic.'

Jason remained stone-faced. 'Do you think he did it to pick up punters? Because that really would be pretty sick.'

'Well, that's what the prosecution argued. Judge gave him eighteen years in the end.' Ray finished his can of drink. 'But no, I don't think so. And I don't think locking him up for eighteen years was ultimately very helpful either. But hey ho.'

At that moment, a young man swung casually round the corner of the street in front of them, loping along with an exaggerated gait. He wore faded grey trainers and blue tracksuit bottoms, which had a white stripe running down each leg. His left arm sported a black, Maori-style tattoo, which wound its way up from his lower arm, disappearing under his grey T-shirt. His head was shaved almost clean whilst his round, baby-like face gleamed in the heat. He was overweight and sweating. As he approached the vehicle, Ray and Jason stepped out of the car. The plump man made no attempt to run, simply turned around and started to shuffle off in the other direction.

'Ian Grant. A word please,' Jason called.

Chapter 2

A young woman squeezed quickly through a hole in the chain link fence and ran towards an old warehouse in an abandoned dockyard. Pulling back a corrugated iron sheet that formed part of the wall, she slipped quietly into the caliginous interior. From under a large cardboard box, a pair of eyes stared out of the darkness. She jogged over to greet them.

'You get it?'

The woman nodded and passed over a small bag containing a white powder.

'What the fuck is that?' His temper exploding, the man jumped up and came for her, raising his right hand. 'I told you, you stupid bitch…'

She backed away, before tripping over her soiled dress and falling. Struggling to get her words out, she rolled onto her back and held her arm up defensively. 'I…I…It's H, it's Ch…Ch…China White.'

The man lowered his hand, uncertain. 'China White?' He paused, glaring at her. His eyes narrowed. 'Where the fuck *d'you* find China White?' he snarled.

She raised herself unsteadily onto a bruised elbow. 'Ch…ch…check it and see.'

The man turned and withdrew back to his cardboard den, sniffing and muttering. Tossing aside a dirty blanket, he picked up a Tupperware food container and a bottle of water, shuffled back out on his knees and sat down on the concrete floor. Motioning the woman over, he opened the box. It held a spoon, a wooden pipe, two disposable lighters, a box of filter tips, a pin, some short lengths of rubber hose and couple of used syringes.

'He said it's very str…str…strong st…stuff.'

The man made no reply. The woman trotted over, sat down opposite him and took an empty coke can from her pocket. Sunlight streamed in through the dirty windows that ran under the ceiling across the southern wall and she held up her chin, the light falling on her face. Then her attention returned to the can, which she dented near the base. Taking the pin from the box, she started to make a series of holes in the dented area.

'You can't chase China White, you dumb bitch.'

She looked up at him, confused. 'Why not?'

'It needs to get too hot. And it's a fucking waste.'

She looked at him, crestfallen. 'Just a little bit? Please?' she implored.

He ignored her for a moment, holding the packet up to the light, staring at it. He glanced across at her, refocussing.

'I can do you a bump, if you want?'

She nodded enthusiastically, smiling at him. She took the water bottle, opened it up and wet her finger, before rubbing the water inside her nasal passage. Then she held out a chewed thumbnail, face-up and tucked into her forefinger, the rest of her hand forming a fist underneath. Grudgingly, the man tapped out a little of the powder, about the size of a match head. She put it to her nose and snorted it, before crawling over to the cardboard den and climbing under the blanket.

The man loosely bound a length of the rubber hose around his right arm and poured a little water into the spoon, followed by a little powder. Then he started to heat the mixture gently with a lighter, swilling it round as he did so. He stared down at it, nodding his approval.

'Looks like good shit.'

He placed a clean filter in the spoon and plunged the syringe into it, before drawing the solution up, slowly, back through the filter tip. Holding the syringe in his right hand, he placed the spoon back onto the plastic lid, ensuring any remaining dregs did not spill. Savagely, he tightened the rubber hose using his teeth and left hand into a makeshift tourniquet and waited, impatiently, for his veins to rise. Switching the syringe into his left hand, he carefully inserted the needle and pushed the solution into his bloodstream.

He closed his eyes and lay back, slowly, onto the concrete, exhaling deeply as he floated away on an opium sea.

Chapter 3

Ian Grant did not turn to face them but continued walking away. The only sign that he had heard at all was an outstretched arm raised behind him, with a single middle finger raised.

'Don't make me run after you Ian, it's too hot,' said Ray, still leaning over the car door. 'And that would really piss me off.'

Ian stopped walking and turned around. 'I ain't done *nothing*. What d'you want? Eh?' His tone was aggressive.

'This is important,' said Ray, walking towards him and lowering his voice as he did so. 'If I wanted to nick you Ian, I would have done it already. I'm not after you. But I haven't sat outside here, sweating my arse off for two hours, for the good of my health.' Ray stopped in his tracks, about ten feet separating the pair of them.

Ian stood, waiting. 'What?'

'Not out here. Get in the car a minute,' said Ray. He turned and walked slowly back to the vehicle. Ian continued to stand on the pavement. Ray opened the driver's door and stopped. 'Please.'

Ian huffed, rolled his eyes, waved his arms and grunted some expletive or other, before moving with surprising alacrity to the parked car and jumping in the back. 'You're taking the piss bruv. I'm not some snout on the payroll, I sold a bit of weed eight months ago. And,' he added with emphasis, 'I got cautioned anyway.'

'Two ounces of skunk and you should have gone down for that and you know it,' said Jason. 'Bagged up, with scales and a bloody firearm.'

'It weren't mine, was it?' glowered Ian. 'We've done this, it's done.' He made to get out of the car but Ray spoke up.

'Look Ian, you do owe me, whether you like it or not is irrelevant. You know full well I got you off that charge by pointing out the technicality on the warrant to your Brief, who wasn't, I grant you, the brightest I have ever come across. And I told you if I wanted to speak to you in the future it would be important. Didn't I tell you that?' There was a brief pause. 'And have I asked you for anything since then?'

Ian considered this in silence. 'We're not friends, bruv.'

Ray glanced swiftly in the rear view mirror to see Ian staring out the passenger window. Now thirty-one years old, Ray had no direct experience in dealing with informants, on any level. Privately educated, he had been brought up in a secure home with middle class values. Both parents had worked hard to ensure that both Ray, and his younger sister, had been given the best possible start in life. However, the family was never cash rich. On the contrary, there had rarely been a ten-pound note in the house and few material possessions of any value.

'So, what you after?' asked Ian, suddenly.

Caught slightly off-guard, Ray did not to let it show. 'I just want to know if any new people have moved into the block recently,' he replied, carefully.

'Council moving people out, not in. Nobody been moved *in* there for years.' Ian smiled.

'Not what I asked Ian.'

Ian continued to study the broken fence. 'Well, nah, not that I seen. I don't know why you need me to answer that anyways, go knock on a fucking door, do some work.'

Ray scratched his head, uncertain whether or not to tell Ian what he was really looking for. Ian, who was no fool, noticed this and read it correctly. Curious as to what CID were doing in this virtually abandoned part of the estate, he seized his opportunity to find out. 'Look, see, you tell me what you really want and I might just help you out. You don't want to level with me…' Ian pulled a face. 'Then I ain't seen nuffin' bruv, d'ya get me?'

Jason looked over at Ray questioningly, but Ray avoided his gaze. He stared straight ahead, poker-faced. 'I can't tell you exactly Ian, as that really would be a direct breach of my orders this morning. I would be very interested to know if you noticed any foreign accents coming from any of the flats recently though. Very interested.' Ray turned suddenly and faced Ian across the car. 'I told you, it's not *you,*' Ray pointed at the flats on the floors legally inhabited by the remaining council tenants, 'that we're after. At least, not right now.' He let this sink in for a moment, safe in the knowledge that Ian was actually quite shrewd. 'You get me?'

Ian did not reply. Inscrutable in the back seat, squinting, his black eyes flicked between the two detectives, assessing them, calculating the threat they posed. Then he spoke.

'Yeah, I get ya. I'll let you know, init.'

Chapter 4

Detective Inspector Rosie Blake stripped quickly out of her clothes, tossing her knickers into the laundry basket with her left foot, before stepping into the shower. She had been on her shift for fourteen hours before the Detective Chief Constable had told her, not unkindly, that she was starting to smell. Gratefully, she had left the building and returned to her small house in Tarnside, a run-down industrial city situated on the southern coast of England. The hot water served as a refreshing tonic, fizzing over her body from the twelve-inch 'Rainshower' head. This was coupled, as recommended, to the German 'Energiesystem' and was a treat that Rosie had installed for herself last year, when she had finally saved enough money to have a modest en suite built over her garage. She had always wanted a giant showerhead with a power system, ever since she was a schoolgirl, and her only regret now was that she had not been able to purchase it sooner.

She closed her eyes and held out an arm against the tiles to steady herself as the hot water beat down upon her shoulders. Her hair was cut in a bob, dark brown in colour which matched her eyes; however, Rosie Blake was not exceptionally beautiful. She kept fit, mainly through swimming, but lacked the high cheekbones and swan-like figure of a conventional beauty. At 5'6", she was more of an acquired taste, with a round face, pale skin and a fairly flat nose, although this was not snub and was reasonably proportioned, as was her mouth. Fairly quiet by nature, she was the type you might initially overlook at a rowdy party. However, men often found her quite alluring, a fact that other women usually found baffling and frequently resented. The upshot of all of this was that Rosie had few female friends, yet was reasonably content in life and felt comfortable in the police force. She had risen through the ranks primarily because she was extremely bright and kept her own counsel. Her experiences with men had been more disappointing;

once the chase was over they had all swiftly dissipated, *like the steam in the bathroom* she had once reflected, in melancholy mood. *Or the Cheshire Cat in Wonderland. Nothing left but the memories of a fading smile.* Currently single, Rosie Blake lived alone.

Stepping out of the shower, she dried herself with a fluffy, white, Egyptian cotton towel. Another treat she had purchased for herself over the past twelve months, this time in the January sales. In fact, she had bought the full Egyptian cotton towel bathroom set. Wary of imitations and having read that Egyptian cotton towels were frequently made with, or only comprised some part of, Egyptian cotton, she had ensured that these were one hundred percent Egyptian cotton and from a reputable store. Again, a purchase she had not regretted, although it had felt rather outrageous at the time.

She walked out from her small en suite into the bedroom, pressed the speakerphone button and listened to the dial tone. The intermittent bleeping told her she had voicemail and she dialled 1571, towelling her hair as she contemplated whether or not to go back to the station tonight to finish up her paperwork. 'You have one new message,' said the recorded voice and she pressed 1 to hear it, before perching on side of the bed. 'Rosie, it's me,' spoke the voice of her boss, Detective Chief Inspector Frank Dowell. 'Don't even think of coming back in this evening, get some sleep and eat something. That's an order. Oh and erm…have a good evening.' There was short pause. 'Well, good night.'

Rosie smiled. That was kind of Frank and unusual. In fact, it was unprecedented, at least as far as she was concerned. She stood, pushed the bathroom door, dropped her towel and examined herself in the full-length mirror screwed into the back of it. 'Looking that bad, huh?' she queried the reflection.

In the mirror, a movement behind her caught her eye and she gasped. 'Oh, I wouldn't say that,' stated a voice, mockingly.

Chapter 5

Rosie snatched up the towel and covered herself. 'What the hell do you want?' she shouted, as outraged as she was frightened. 'How dare you come in here, what are you, some kind of perv?'

'Ha. Don't flatter yourself,' the man sneered. There was a moment's pause. Rosie glanced at the phone. 'Don't do anything stupid,' said the man.

He was dressed in black: black balaclava, black polo jumper, black leather gloves, black trousers, black trainers with black soles. 'You now have two choices,' said the voice. 'You can get dressed, come downstairs and get in the back of the van. Or I knock you out, carry you downstairs and throw you in it. Choose.'

The seconds felt like minutes. Rosie felt her stomach tighten a notch with every tick of the bedroom clock. She swallowed hard, trying to maintain control of her emotions. She wanted to cry and fight all at once. And at the same time she felt very confused. She tried to speak but involuntarily stammered. 'W...why?'

'Don't know. Boss wants to meet you.'

'Is he...going to hurt me?'

'Don't know, don't think so.'

'Fuck.'

'No.'

Suddenly, Rosie realized the man was foreign. She was not offering to sleep her way out of this!

'Dressed is better but...' the man shrugged. 'Up to you.'

Rosie wanted to think clearly, assess the situation, give herself sensible options, but her mind was racing and fear tightened round her like a noose. There was nothing in here that would make any sort of weapon, this was a bedroom not a kitchen. She looked around desperately. Slippers, make-up, a dressing gown...Maybe in the bathroom there were some nail scissors. She needed time, time to think.

'Okay,' said Rosie. She hesitated again, trying desperately to quell the panic that kept rising out of her stomach and grabbing at her throat.

The man looked at the clock, ticking on her bedside table, before speaking. 'You have six minutes before the bomb under your bed will explode. Clothes here.' He tossed her a plastic bag. 'Dress or come naked.' She remained frozen to the spot, terrified. She felt tears in her eyes. The man must be completely insane. Why had he suddenly materialised here, in her most private space? Suddenly he raised his arm angrily and stepped towards her. 'Do it, NOW!'

At the sound of his sudden shouting, she wet herself. Then she started to whimper. Seeing the woman was close to hysteria, the man spoke quietly again. 'Just get dressed please. Five minutes. In two minutes I have to hurt you. Dress. Now.'

Without another word, Rosie snatched up the bag and went into the bathroom. 'You stay where I can see you,' he threatened, coming after her.

'Just fuck off and let me wash a minute,' she sobbed, turning the bathroom taps and using the shower accessory. Disgusted with herself, embarrassed, ashamed and humiliated, she washed the pee down the plughole and dried herself. She stalked back into the bedroom stark naked and, suddenly, furiously angry. 'You like to watch do you, little man. You fucking little prick.' She dressed swiftly, bra, pants, a white cotton blouse, black pencil skirt. 'These are my own clothes, you little wanker.'

'Yes.'

'Why are you giving me my own clothes in a fucking bag?' She held the empty bag out questioningly, quivering through a combination of fear and adrenaline.

'Quicker. Shoes by the front door. Move.'

He hustled her downstairs and over to the front door. As she buckled on her most sensible shoes the man took something from his back pocket, a syringe stuck into a cork. Rosie glanced up and caught sight of it in his hand.

'NO!'

'You stand slowly. We walk to van, you climb in. Otherwise...' he nodded at the syringe in his left hand. 'Very dangerous. No noise.' He waited for her to stand up. 'I don't like to use this but the boss, he don't like guns. Don't be stupid please.'

Standing behind her, the man gripped her shoulder firmly with his left hand and she felt the side of the needle pushing gently against her skin. The sensation made her neck prickle. Holding this position, the syringe concealed beneath her hair, the man opened the front door with his right hand. Pushing her forward, he pulled the door shut behind him and walked casually out of the end of terrace house, steering Rosie to the back door of a battered, blue transit van. Maintaining his grip, he swung open the van door with his right hand and waited.

In that moment, Rosie thought of crying out for help, of ducking away from her attacker, of running away. The back of the van was dimly lit by a small, flat light in the ceiling. It looked cramped and dirty. The grip on her neck tightened and started to hurt. She climbed in and sat on the bench that ran along the left-hand side of the interior, watching helplessly as the door swung quietly shut behind her.

Chapter 6

The metal doors were wrenched open.

'Out, please.'

Rosie stepped down meekly from the van, stretching her back as she stood and rolling her shoulders back. For approximately three hours she had been sitting on the wooden slats that comprised the makeshift bench in the back of the van. Most of the drive had been straight and at speed, but the last forty minutes had been in traffic. She had heard the noise of the vehicles outside when they had been held up: lorries chugging, the harsh gasp of double decker buses, muffled shouting and swearing. London voices.

Now, she was in a double garage comprised of standard grey breezeblocks, a strip light hung overhead and a single door was visible off to the left. The silence was deafening.

'You wait here.' The man walked swiftly towards the door and knocked on it. He was still wearing his balaclava, which he had, Rosie presumed, taken off for the long drive. Now more composed, she wondered how many CCTV cameras they may have passed on the way here. If she could just get the registration plates then it might be possible to check at a later date. Her abductor turned back towards her. 'Don't move, don't think about moving, don't think about escaping or trying anything. You might need to sleep here first.'

'First?' she enquired.

'Before you meet boss.' He paused a moment, before shrugging. 'I don't know,' he admitted.

Clearly, this was as far as his orders had gone. That much was obvious. She was still having problems placing the accent as well, it sounded like some sort of weird cross between Italian and Russian.

'Have you blown up my house?'

The man laughed. 'Don't be stupid. Nobody want to blow up your house.'

At that moment, the door opened and another man in similar dress came into the garage, a balaclava also covering his face. He spoke calmly and quietly with her abductor for about three minutes. He glanced over at Rosie a few times and then motioned to her to come forward. Her abductor walked out of the garage through the open door and was gone.

'Rosie Blake?' This man unmistakably hailed from south London but his accent was polished, middle class. 'Sorry about the transport arrangements but I needed to see you. You're not hurt, are you?'

'No,' she replied, adding, 'I see your man waited until I was in the shower.'

The figure laughed. 'I knew that would piss you off. That's why I sent B to come and fetch you. He's completely asexual, I assure you. You know what that means, right?'

'A person who has no interest in sex.'

'Correct. He has absolutely no sex drive whatsoever. For either sex I might add.' He walked towards her and stood opposite a few yards away, hands on hips. 'I am afraid waiting until you were naked was my idea. As a trained and experienced officer, I needed to ensure you were in the most vulnerable state possible, in case you tried to be a hero. Or heroine, in your case.'

He stood, studying her for a minute. He was quite unreadable and Rosie felt her shoulders tensing. His stare was unnerving. She felt quite out of her depth. 'He also informs me you offered to sleep with him to avoid meeting me.' The man drew closer to Rosie and his emerald-green eyes glistened through the slit in his balaclava. 'That is a disappointment.'

'Ha' she snorted, drawing her head back slightly. 'Your man is a gibbering idiot.' The man withdrew, and stood opposite her once again, adopting the same pose as before. 'When he suddenly appeared in my room and threatened me, I said "Fuck". His response, to my exclamation of shock and surprise, was "No".'

Unexpectedly, the man exploded with laughter at this revelation. He threw his head back and let rip with a deep, throaty, chest-heaving laugh. For a few moments, he struggled to regain his composure. 'Oh, that's priceless. Seriously.' He wiped a tear from his eye.

Rosie did not know what to make of any of it. This conversation was completely bizarre, surreal. She struggled to gain a handle on it. 'What do you want? Why am I here?'

'I'm sorry, we've been having a bit of a party tonight. I would invite you through but, well...the party is almost over.' Keeping his eyes on her, he took a walkie-talkie from his pocket and held it to his mouth. 'Two chairs in the garage please. Quickly. Cover up.'

He was all business now, the smiles had evaporated and his eyes locked onto hers with a deliberate, controlled intensity. Rosie stared straight back at them, trying to hide how frightened she felt, standing tall. His eyes did not look emerald-green anymore. The pupils were larger and the outskirts of the irises had turned a colder shade of turquoise, flashing hints of spearmint blue. 'Now,' he said, softly, his voice iced with menace. 'I do hope you're going to co-operate.'

Chapter 7

So far, Ray was privately quite pleased with the new recruit to the CID section. He thought Jason was a good copper and felt he had the potential to become a good detective. Frank had assigned Jason to work his first case under Ray after some deliberation, the timing fortuitously coinciding with a brand new investigation. 'It's important', Frank had advised.

As of three days ago, Ray was part of Operation Virtus, an overarching, UK-wide, National Crime Agency operation being run in conjunction with the Serious Organised Crime Agency (SOCA) and the Border Police that had, in turn, been directly commissioned by the Home Office. Illegal immigration was a particularly hot potato in the current political climate and with elections looming in the next eight months it appeared that the government had, according to Frank, 'got a real bee in its bonnet' on the issue. 'Don't be a lone wolf on this one, Ray,' he had warned. 'Nobody will thank you for it, least of all me. There's no lack of resources available and I *need* to be kept informed. On top of all the bureaucracy we normally have to contend with these days, the Divisional Commander and the Chief Inspector are breathing down the Superintendent's neck, so you can work out how that falls down the chain. You can bet that they will want everything done by the book. And if we are assigned an external DSI at any stage, I will expect your full and unreserved co-operation this time.'

This last comment had referred to the Detective Superintendent that Ray had last been instructed to work under. Detective Superintendent officers are never in charge of divisional CID (a job that belongs to the Detective Chief Inspector), but are commonly in charge of any outside investigation teams who may be called in for very special circumstances, such as the hunting of a serial killer.

For a multitude of reasons, Ray had hated the last Detective Superintendent he had been forced to work under, a woman who had been assigned to their division on a temporary attachment. He had also bitterly resented her interference in what Ray had considered to be 'his case'. He had, therefore, deliberately failed to keep her, or the department, informed at any stage and had worked almost entirely alone for two months. This would not have bothered Frank quite as much, had Ray not simultaneously kept the Detective Superintendent chasing shadows by feeding her cryptic information; a fact she had then formally complained about, resulting in Frank having his ears severely scorched by the Superintendent. Somewhat fortuitously, Ray had managed to bring the operation to a successful conclusion literally hours before a scheduled meeting and had thus managed to circumvent Frank's wrath, who had been planning to erupt on him that very day in spectacular fashion. The following day, Ray had taken two weeks leave to the south of France and had since arrived back from his holiday, less than a week ago.

Within days of his return he had been summoned to meet with the Detective Chief Inspector, who told Ray with an unnerving calm precisely how unhappy he was with the manner in which Ray had gone about his work over the past two months. Frank had then, begrudgingly, admitted that it had been a good result.

However, still fuming that he had been forced to bear the brunt of the Superintendent's wrath for Ray's persistent insubordination, Frank denied to inform Ray in private of his plans for the new CID recruit. Instead, he interrupted their meeting to call a complete stranger into his office and then played his ace card, springing the news while Ray's new lackey sat alongside him in the form of Detective Constable Jason Stephenson.

Initially, it had the intended effect of infuriating Ray who had, much to Frank's satisfaction, slowly turned a darker shade of red as he sat, stone-faced, whilst the official brief was outlined to the pair of them. Frank made no bones about the need to respect the chain of command, highlighting the point by glaring at the pair of them in turn and jabbing his desk with a fat forefinger. As intended, Jason thought this little side-show was primarily for his benefit but Frank was a shrewd operator, his choice of words leaving Ray in no doubt that his antics on the last case were still far from forgiven.

'That's *information*,' Frank had emphasised, glaring briefly at Ray. 'Pulling in ten illegals and banging them up in the nick for example, does not constitute a result.' Frank had sat back in his chair at this point and proceeded to speak calmly and clearly, as was his normal manner.

'Operation Virtus has a single objective. To close down the criminal gangs bringing people into the country and from the top down. We are *not* after the odd driver or hired thug here, you could blow the whole operation. What we do need is a full understanding of the chain of command and any action, ANY action, that you feel may be necessary is to be reported to DI Beattie in the normal manner and then it must be approved by me. No Wild West antics, thank you.

'Once we have all the information we can gather, then we will be bringing them all in, across the country, in a series of co-ordinated, dawn raids. I hope you understand the need for transparency here? I will not stand for being the only division that fails to fall in line, or is seen to be acting like some sort of maverick. And I can't possibly protect anybody who fails to respect this. Heads WILL roll. I can't make this any plainer. This is a joint, co-ordinated effort across multiple divisions. Clear?'

Both men had indicated their assent, before the lecture had continued. They were not informed as to whether or not Operation Virtus formed part of a broader, European investigation, but Ray privately doubted it. Despite public claims to the contrary, the current front bench comprising the elected government were predominately euro-sceptic. Given the various organisations, agencies and police units that had been mobilised, Ray felt it far more likely the government was operating off their own initiative, rather than solely assisting with some obligatory European agenda or directive. He mused that it was still possible that Interpol, or some foreign agency, was involved at a higher level.

Chapter 8

The young woman rubbed her eyes, staring out blearily at a gloomy world. The high having passed, an overwhelming sadness rushed in to fill the void. An emptiness. Slipping her hand into her pocket, she retrieved a pocket mirror. It was too dark to see herself. Cold, she gathered the blanket around herself and clambered out slowly from the cardboard box. She managed a few steps, before sitting down heavily in a sunlit patch of concrete to look at her reflection. Dirt was smeared down the left-hand side of her face from where she had passed out. She spat on the sleeve of her purple, corduroy shirt and tried to rub it away. Dark, black circles surrounded her sockets, black holes in a sallow face. Misery enveloping her, she put the mirror back in her pocket. Abruptly, she turned and retched violently onto the blanket.

She looked up quickly, frightened, but the man was still passed out on the floor. He was going to beat her for this, no question. Puking on his blanket. She was so stupid, he told her so all the time. Stupid bitch. Dumb bitch. Now she had done it again, another stupid thing.

Wobbling unsteadily, she went over to where he lay and started to cry. She lay down next to him and put a hand on his chest. He felt very cold. She lay there for a few seconds before noticing his chest was not moving. Panicking, she sat up, grabbed the lapels of his jacket and shook him. He did not respond. Frantically, she grabbed the lighter from the box and flicked the metal roller. Nothing happened, but she kept trying, until a small flame spurted from the plastic skin. She held it to his face.

His eyes were closed and he looked serenely calm, his mouth turned upwards in a faint smile; but his lips were pale and his face was ashen.

Scrambling to her feet, she started to back away. She must find somebody, an ambulance. Maybe he was okay? She had heard of it before, the heartbeat slowing down and people assuming the worst, when really it was just a little OD. But she must get help, fast!

Her heart pounding, adrenaline started flooding through her system. She turned and ran from the warehouse, pushing through the corrugated sheet, out into the bright sunlight and across the concrete, squeezing through the fence. Sprinting down Old Street, she saw a police car, parked up, blocking the street where the shops were. Panting, she paused. She had spent the last year of her life avoiding them.

Then the image of the man, pale, still, prone, flashed through her mind and she ran towards the patrol vehicle shouting, eyes brimming with tears, shouting about the warehouse, the old docks, they must get help; but suddenly her head swam and she felt herself falling, consumed by the darkness, collapsing straight into the outstretched arms of PC Lucy Greene.

***

Detective Chief Inspector Frank Dowell sat on his leather-bound chair behind the steel desk in his small, glass-fronted office, sweating profusely. A three-drawer filing cabinet was in the opposite corner to his left and a large fan perched there, precariously situated on top of a bundle of paper files. It swept round the office slowly and anything remotely paper-like had been weighted down with a book, stapler or whatever had come to hand. Frank was a big fella, weighing in at twenty-one stone, a former prop forward in his youth and built like an apple barrel. He was a cheerful and popular man, a seasoned detective who had risen through the ranks slowly and doggedly. Unlike many officers nowadays, he had spent almost his entire working life at the one police station and he was quite a well-known figure in Tarnside, having handled the occasional press conference over the years.

Right now, however, he felt unbearably hot. His shirt, pressing against him in damp, wet, sticky patches, was playing havoc with his eczema; thus aside from the insufferable heat, he was also unbearably itchy. He threw his pen down on the desk. This was intolerable! He felt like an army of red ants were burrowing into his right arm. He seized his shirt with both hands and looked skyward. For a moment, he almost gave into the temptation to rip the darn thing off. He stood up, intending to fetch himself a cold can of drink from the vending machine in the corridor. At that precise moment there was a knock on the door, which was open; however, the knocker hung back, out of sight.

'Yes?' said Frank, testily. 'Don't hide out there man, what is it?'

Police Constable Lucy Greene entered his office. 'Sorry Sir, I was asked to bring this to your office, by DI Fairbairn?'

'Right, yes, thank you.'

Lucy stood, unsure where exactly to place the paper file containing various colour photocopies and documents. Frank was now seated back behind his desk, elbows on the table, head in his hands, eyes closed. This was awkward.

'We have a body, guv. An OD down at the docks and a young woman in hospital. Would you like me to go down and take a statement?'

'No, thank you,' he replied. 'It's a job for a DC.' Frank looked up and held his hand out for the file. He fixed a penetrating stare on her for a moment. 'Have you ever thought of moving into CID, PC Greene?'

Lucy, having had no idea that the Detective Chief Inspector even knew her name, was taken completely unawares. She replied coolly, 'I have thought about it, guv, yes, more so recently.'

'Good,' said Frank. 'Do it. That will be all.'

He took the file from her hand and Lucy ducked swiftly out of the office. Lifting a mug, he slid the file into his 'Inbox' without opening it and checked the time on his computer. It was only 10.55 and he was due a catch-up with one of his Detective Inspectors this morning at 11.00. He had thought it was Rosie, but, given the file that had been dropped into his lap, maybe it was Mark after all? He checked his online calendar; no, it was definitely Detective Inspector Rosie Blake this morning.

Frank reflected bitterly that he only had himself to blame for the paperwork scattered about his office. He hated reading off a screen and then switching from one photo to another and then back to the relevant word file, or case note, or witness statement, in fact the whole practice had driven him crazy. After a few years of battling with it, he had stipulated that all case files were to be printed out, in full, and handed to him in the 'old school' format. The electronic copies were all saved on the network's shared drive and each file password protected, but Frank rarely bothered to access them by that medium. He liked to compare forensic notes, statements, photos and so forth, side by side and he had argued, successfully as it turned out, that there was no substitute for this. In truth, he had met little resistance from the Superintendent, whose remit stated solely that case files were to be stored electronically on an encrypted, shared, network drive. The detailed security aspects of the IT set-up remained well beyond his comprehension. The Superintendent told Frank that so long as the electronic records were maintained, he was free to kill as many trees as he saw fit in the line of duty.

The due hour came, but no Detective Inspector Blake arrived at his office, which surprised Frank a great deal. He remembered sending her home the previous evening, so she should have had a decent rest and he could not fathom why she had failed to attend. With more reminders these days that one could shake a stick at, in the form of mobile phones and laptops and emails, it seemed highly unlikely she would have forgotten her monthly meeting with the Head of Department. He pondered that perhaps she had been taken ill; she had looked pretty rough yesterday in truth. Even so, it seemed strange she had not simply rung and told him directly. Perplexed, he rang her mobile number but it rang to answerphone, as did her house number. He declined to leave a message. Further enquiries around the station also proved fruitless. Rosie Blake was nowhere to be found.

Chapter 9

Tarnside is an ugly, sprawling, hotchpotch of buildings that worms its way across a mile of the southern coastline, marring its face like a cicatrix. Once a busy, working port, the old industrialised area to the east remains a mass of old buildings, warehouses and disused machinery, surrounded by a chain link fence and topped with barbed wire set upon inward-pointing, metal struts. Cheaply constructed shortly after the millennium, private apartment blocks are untidily stacked up around it, contrasting starkly with the dilapidated Victorian structures spread out beneath them. Hemmed in between the abandoned dockyards and adjacent red light district, many of these flats had failed to sell and already looked tired, despite never having housed an occupant, their once pristine, white exteriors stained with grime and bird excrement.

The city centre received the bulk of the budget assigned by the government for regeneration and the main thoroughfare, Union Street, is now pedestrianized. The traffic that once crawled through here now winds its way around the eastern side of it, redirected via a costly dual carriageway littered with pelican crossings and incorporating a pink bus lane, used primarily by various taxi firms. The dual carriageway wends its way down to the coast, where the two lanes merge into a roundabout known as the 'Crooked Billet', in memory of the public house that had remained there for many years, derelict and in splendid isolation, before it was eventually pulled down. The roundabout was as far as the allocated budget had stretched and thus Union Street, usually now simply referred to as the high street, remains surrounded by a variety of random buildings, busy roads, residential streets and back alleys. Many of these routes are now one-way and double parked, ensuring traffic jams and arguments remain a permanent feature of life. The shops on Union Street come and go on a regular basis, the most timeless feature being a McDonald's that has been in situ since 1978.

From the Crooked Billet roundabout the two main routes are either east, down Old Street towards the old docks, or west, along The Esplanade. The Esplanade runs parallel to the coastline and is initially hemmed in by double-storey buildings, their ground floors a mixture of fast-food outlets, curry houses and off-licences, punctuated by estate agents and specialist shops such as 'Mike's Bikes'. The road is eventually intercepted by a mini-roundabout which marks the start of the 'Pebble Hill' district, once a separate village entirely but long since swallowed up into the sprawling mass of Tarnside. The Esplanade then proceeds at a modest acclivity, opening out onto a communal grassy knoll that rolls gently down to a stretch of pebbled beach.

Ray was driving down Old Street with Jason in an unmarked black Audi, one of the CID pool cars. Since leaving the station, Ray had been moaning to Jason about his disastrous holiday and how rude everybody in France had been to him whilst he was there. In addition, he had slated the food, the poor hotel accommodation, the blatant racism he had witnessed to beggars on the street and the general cost of living. Having now followed the road for some distance, an apparently endless, corrugated iron fence running along their right-hand side, Ray was now articulating that it was little wonder every immigrant in Europe could not leave the country fast enough. He confided in Jason that, by the end of his trip, he had been of a similar mind-set. Ahead, two gates formed a split in the fencing, both held open with a couple of bricks. The large metal frames were covered with the same corrugated iron wire that made up the rest of the old fence. Upon entering the abandoned dockyard, Ray reflected what a vast area lay there on the seafront, wasting away.

Finally, after following numerous traffic cones, Ray pulled up at the scene. A squad car, a forensics van and two unmarked vehicles were already assembled outside one of the warehouses. The divisional surgeon emerged from the building, striding across the concrete as Ray cut the engine.

'Shouldn't take long,' Ray stated quietly to Jason, 'then we'll get over to the hospital and take a statement. See if we can find out who supplied it.'

***

Rosie Blake was imprisoned in a cool cellar, dimly lit by a low wattage bulb. She was not hurt or bound and she was lying on a red sofa with gold, swirling patterns embossed into its cushions, which had little red tassels running along the length of them. It looked like it had once been rather plush. In addition to the sofa, there were two, large, matching armchairs and a battered walnut coffee table that was fixed crudely to the floor, the base of each leg swathed with some type of cement or mortar. On the coffee table was a toilet roll, an un-opened bottle of mineral water and some digestive biscuits. Aside from this, she had found a clean blanket on the sofa upon her arrival and a bucket in the corner, lined with a white, plastic bag.

Her conversation last night had been fairly brief. She knew absolutely nothing about Operation Virtus. She had not been threatened or hurt. After ten minutes or so, the man had instructed her to place the cloth bag over her head, before escorting her from the garage and into the cellar. He had then stated that someone would speak with her again in the morning. His parting shot had been that he hoped, for her sake, that her memory would clear with some sleep.

Rosie had slept fitfully, her mind whirring. Now lying awake on the sofa, she remembered wetting herself and felt heat creeping back into her face. She flushed, closing her eyes, but all the terrifying emotions that had accompanied the moment came rushing back, welling up through her body like a tidal wave, flooding her thoughts and senses and roaring through her head. Hot tears pricked her eyelids. She scrunched them tightly in response, fighting to regain control. *Bastards.*

A harsh grating sound broke the silence, followed by two clangs, implying two external bolts had been drawn back. She sat up sharply as the steel door slowly opened. A man stood silhouetted at the top of the stairs, fists clenched by his sides, the light behind him casting long shadows into the basement. He stood there, silently, for about twenty seconds, the effect creating a black hole where his face should have been. Then he laughed at her, a nasty, spiteful laugh.

This was a laugh she did not recognise from last night; it was high pitched, giggling and splenetic. Despite herself, she found it unnerving. When the man spoke his tone was also abnormally high in pitch. 'And this little piggy went...wee wee wee all the way home.'

Chapter 10

Above all else, Rosie possessed sharp instincts and every sense in her body was screaming at her to get out of there right now and as fast as humanly possible. But escape was not possible.

She watched fearfully as he came down the stairs, taking off his black leather gloves as he did so. When he next spoke his voice was quiet, menacing.

'Hello little piggy. You want to see my face little piggy? You want to see me?'

She turned her face away, refusing to look at him. He grabbed her chin with one hand and held her tightly, pushing his fingers into her cheeks whilst she stared away from him. 'You know the good cop, bad cop routine, right? Of course you do, that's how you fit people up, isn't it, that old drill! So let's see how you like being on the receiving end of your own game, little piggy. Now, let's play. You're the suspect...' he paused, releasing his grip and backing off a few feet. 'Now, guess who I want to play?'

There was a horrible pause. Rosie remained silent, looking away. The man put one foot on the coffee table and leant over his prisoner.

'I'd like to kill you, piggy,' he whispered to her, his voice filled with hatred. 'I'd like to stick barbed fishing hooks into your eyes and slowly rip out your eyeballs while you sit there, tied down and screaming. There's so many things I would enjoy doing to a PIG' he spat out the word, 'like you.' He shifted position and stood back from her. Silence hung in the air for a few seconds, before he swiftly rounded the coffee table, placed one hand on the sofa arm and leant down until his face was just a foot or so from her own. 'Now listen up, piggy. This is your very...last...chance. What do you know about the Operation Virtus?'

Rosie turned her face to look at him. These eyes were smoky brown, fiery, angry. Rage simmered in those eyes, something wild, unharnessed. It frightened her. In her gap year, Rosie had visited an active volcano in Hawaii and staring down into the fiery pit was one of her clearest memories. *Is this what madness looks like?*

'I don't know anything about it. I have never even heard of it. I don't know who you people are or why you have singled me out.'

The man considered her in silence for moment before withdrawing, slowly. He folded his arms and stood opposite her, the coffee table between them.

'Have you even considered that I might be telling the truth?' Rosie suddenly slammed the arm of the sofa in frustration. 'I don't know anything about it. What the hell is Operation Virtus? Why don't *you* tell *me*? If you release me then I'm going to make a point of finding out and otherwise,' her voice wavered. She closed her eyes and took a deep breath. 'Well, otherwise, it doesn't make a lot of difference, does it?'

The man did not flinch. He let the question hang in the air for a moment before replying. 'Maybe I'll release you with your tongue cut out.'

'That won't stop me using a keyboard, will it?'

In one motion, the man stood swiftly over the coffee table, raised his arm back and slapped her, hard, across the face. 'Don't push me bitch.'

It was the first real, physical violence that Rosie had ever been on the end of and it hurt. Angry, red marks showed up instantly across her left cheek where his fingers had struck her. The pain was sharp, brutal and unexpected and it shook her, tears once again welling up from deep inside, which she brushed away with hot fingers.

'In fact, you just keep pushing,' he snarled at her. 'Make my day.'

A long shadow appeared on the stairs. Rosie looked up to see another man standing there, looking down on them both.

***

'Wait here,' said Ray to Jason. He exited the vehicle and walked briskly over to where Detective Inspector Mark Fairbairn was standing at the entrance to the warehouse. He was greeted with a grunt.

'There's not much to see,' said Mark. 'I'm having forensics take the body for an autopsy as soon as they arrive.'

'Uh-huh,' Ray replied. There was a brief pause before Mark suddenly turned on Ray.

'Why are *you* here, anyway?' he demanded. 'Did Frank send you?'

Mark was imposing, standing at 6'4" and broad across the chest. He had hazel eyes and sported a mass of untidy, brown, curly hair. His full beard was much darker in colour than his hair and flecked with grey. Ray had heard a few of the Constables quietly refer to him as 'Little John', after the fabled character of the Robin Hood legends.

Mark stared down at the junior ranking officer suspiciously and Ray promptly proceeded to smile back. 'Yes,' he replied. 'DI Blake has gone AWOL. And I know you're up to your eyes in that jewellery racket at the moment.'

'Rosie has gone AWOL?'

'Well she didn't turn up for her meeting with the DCI this morning. I take it you've not been in today?'

'Only briefly,' Mark replied. 'Is that why I'm here? Waste of my bloody time. You want this, you can have it as far as I'm concerned.'

'Right ho,' said Ray, popping a mint into this mouth.

Ray's bonhomie was in sharp contrast to Mark's frame of mind. Glancing over to the pool car and seeing Jason in the front seat did little to improve his mood. Already aggravated that Ray appeared to be at a loose end whilst he was being requested to spread himself more thinly by the hour, it now transpired his junior had been assigned an extra man who was, evidently, sat about doing nothing useful either.

'Well, I certainly have more important things to be getting on with,' he snapped.

Ray's next comment was akin to water on a hotplate. He proffered his packet to Mark. 'Mint?'

Mark glared down at him, angrily. 'No I don't want a fucking mint!' He took a deep breath, extracted car keys from his pocket and started walking. 'I'll leave it in your capable hands,' he called back. 'Witness statement. Crime scene report. You know the drill. I'll speak to Frank, but until he says otherwise I remain the SIO. So don't fuck it up.'

Ray watched him get into his car before turning round and ambulating back to the Vauxhall. He went round to Jason's side and indicated to him to wind down the window. Jason shrugged helplessly and then Ray recalled that the windows were electric and the car keys in his pocket. He appeared to have absentmindedly locked the doors. He pressed the fob and Jason clambered out, his forehead damp with sweat.

'Like a bloody oven in there,' he remarked. 'What kept you?'

'Oh, just sharing a bit of banter with DI Fairbairn,' Ray replied.

They started walking into the warehouse towards the body, where the police photographer was finishing his shots.

'Mint?' Ray held the packet out to him.

'Oh, no thanks,' Jason replied.

'You sure?' Ray queried. 'They don't completely drown out the death smell. But they do help.'

Chapter 11

The young woman awoke in hospital, clothed in a white gown. She closed her eyes again and swallowed, but her mouth felt dry and her tongue swollen. She coughed quietly. As if by magic, a nurse appeared by her side and asked her how she was feeling.

She saw a tube in her arm, an intravenous drip. She croaked her response, 'Not great.'

The nurse helped her to prop herself up and drink a little water before she spoke again, telling her the police would want to ask her some questions but she was not in any trouble. Did she know her name?

'Ellie,' she said. 'What happened to Mike?'

The nurse shook her head. 'If you mean the man in the warehouse, he didn't make it. I'm sorry.'

Ellie closed her eyes and lay back. The nurse touched her shoulder gently and turned briskly away, pulling the curtains shut around her and promising to be back soon. Ellie nodded. The nurse gone, Ellie's eyes filled with tears. She turned onto her side and wept, until, eventually, she fell asleep.

***

Dressed in the familiar black, self-styled uniform the men had apparently adopted, the man spoke loudly, projecting his voice down the steps. His voice was unmistakably foreign, the words clipped. Frustratingly, Rosie realized she still could not place the accent.

'Operation Virtus is an operation being conducted by your government, in conjunction with various UK agencies such as the National Crime Agency and including, of course, the Tarnside police force. It is a subject of particular interest to my people.' He walked casually down the steps and motioned to her aggressor to leave the room with a hand gesture. The man immediately complied, taking the steps two at a time.

'He was not meant to hurt you, simply to frighten you. Rest assured, he will be punished.'

It really is the good cop, bad cop routine. And to be fair, they are pretty good at it.

'Now the fact that you clearly know nothing about it, is a serious problem. I had always intended to release you, completely unharmed, if you co-operated. Once we understood what your force currently knew, we planned to move things around and then let you go home.'

'So this was all about staying one step ahead?'

'Precisely DI Blake. Nothing personal. Just business. I am not some common criminal. In fact, I help people. I am, what do you call it…' he searched for the relevant word before pointing at the sky triumphantly, 'Ah yes! Humanitarian.'

Rosie had often been told her face revealed too much. Her jaw actually dropped at this statement and she looked over to him from her seat on the sofa, her visage a mixture of disgust and scornful derision. Disregarding the danger she was in for a moment, she stated simply, 'Come again?'

'You think this is bad, DI Blake?'

Rosie could see that her words had angered him. She kept silent and looked down at the floor. His voice still raised a notch, the man continued.

'Is the sofa not to your taste? Are your cushions uncomfortable? Did we omit to wash your blanket in Non-Biological washing powder?' He paced a few steps and simmered down, before facing her over the coffee table. When he next spoke, his body language was open and it was with hand gestures and passion. He carried an air of relaxed authority.

'At least you are not spending forty-eight hours in a suitcase. Or thirteen days in a freezer lorry. Your life is not so wretched that you are attempting to row your family across an ocean in a four-foot rubber dinghy, designed for rich children to play in at the seaside when they tire of their picnics and ice creams.

'There is no fear, for your people, of waking up to find your own child lying dead alongside you tomorrow, frozen to death. Because, in your attempt to give them a better life, you failed to protect them, failed to give them enough to eat, to keep them warm enough; so they perished while you slept between crates under the plastic sheet that you told them was home. Eating from bins, skulking like an animal, bringing up your children in a car park amongst thieves and paedophiles and murderers. Then, staring at the corpse that was your child, you have to ask yourself; was it really a better life for them you wanted? Or was that just what *you* wanted? Now, can you imagine living with that kind of guilt, Detective Inspector?'

Rosie looked up. 'No, I can't,' she stated, simply.

He stood, studying her for a moment, weight evenly distributed on both feet, arms folded, right over left. Then he shifted position, switching the bulk of his weight onto his left foot. Bringing his right hand to his chin, he started gently tapping his mouth, thoughtfully. She waited for him to continue.

'Human life is not valued in the same way everywhere.' His arms reverted to the crossed position. 'The loss of one life, in order to save many more, is the obvious choice. You may become an indirect casualty, incidentally, of the wars your government has started. Considering the service I provide, that would be quite an irony.'

'You're a people trafficker.'

'Not really DI Blake. That's just a term your government chooses to adopt when trying to vilify people like me. People risking their own freedom to help innocents escape the reality of their ugly power struggles. You do remember your government invading Iraq, for example? Afghanistan? I want us to be quite clear.'

'I remember.'

'Good.' He stood up straight suddenly, pushing his shoulders back. 'I have made a decision. You will stay here, until I can move you somewhere else. For now,' he indicated the bucket, 'you will have to make do.'

He turned to leave the room, but then pivoted back to face her again. 'I am not, fortunately for you, in the business of hurting innocents. I dare say you find that hard to believe but, believe me, this is a tough business.' He paused for a moment and locked eyes with her. Blue eyes. 'To howl with the wolves is an excuse of those who bleat with the sheep.'

Then he turned on his heel and started slowly up the stairs. 'Don't feel sorry for yourself, DI Blake. Just think on what we spoke about.'

The steel door swung shut. Metal grated on metal.

Chapter 12

Ray had left Jason at the scene to oversee the removal of the body to the morgue, whilst he planned to go and speak with the girl who had run into PC Lucy Greene. The report crackled in as Ray started the engine.

'This is Delta Whisky calling all units, we have a suspected three one one on Clifton Street, requesting immediate response, over.'

Ray grabbed the radio.

'This is India Juliett one five two, can you repeat, is that a three one one, over?'

'India Juliett one five two, Delta Whisky confirms that it is a suspected three one one, repeat, a suspected three one one, can you attend, over?'

'India Juliett one five two, confirm I can attend Clifton Street, ETA three minutes, over.'

'Thank you India Juliett one five two, message received, head to thirteen Clifton Street 'Fresh and Salty', be advised we also have Tango Tango three six four and Tango Tango four one eight on their way, ETA thirteen minutes, let us know if you need anything, over.'

Ray sped off from the warehouse and roared across the concrete, swinging out onto the main road. Flicking on the blues hidden behind the radiator grille and gunning the Audi up the street the speedometer raced into life, briefly touching sixty-five, before Ray slowed down, knowing that he was definitely in the vicinity. Finding Clifton Street shortly before he reached the Crooked Billet roundabout, he swung right, driving on for another hundred metres or so before pulling over. A small row of shops lay to the left, behind a parched patch of grass and a marginally broader expanse of pavement. In contrast to the run down terraced houses hemming them in, the parade was set back slightly from the roadside.

Ray grabbed a notebook from the glove compartment and jumped out of the vehicle, stuffing it into his back pocket as did so. A small crowd of onlookers was gathered by the window, a few of whom were cupping their hands over their faces and peering inside. Others stood about, shrugging and looking generally bemused. Ray wondered why none of them were at work.

'Police, stand back please,' said Ray authoritatively, holding his police ID card up clearly at head height whilst marching towards the chip shop. The dozen or so onlookers made little attempt to move, with only the three nearest the door shuffling back a few feet. 'Who called the police?' Ray demanded.

A portly man in his fifties, sporting a grubby white T-Shirt and knee length grey shorts, volunteered his hand like a schoolboy. He came forward to where Ray was standing and spoke in hushed tones. 'I think he's dead.'

'How so?' Ray replied, walking smartly towards the narrow take-away.

The battered, wooden door had once been sky blue, but the paint had mostly flaked away now, revealing a creamy undercoat. Above the lower panel was a large window, behind which a yellow, discoloured blind was suspended, firmly closed. A lopsided sign hung on the door, displaying the opening hours. The shop front itself followed the same pattern as the door, consisting primarily of a glass front that ran down to within three foot of the pavement. Below this, it was apparent that the concrete had once been the same sky blue colour, but it was now mainly cream.

'Stand BACK!' Ray angrily demanded, startling those nearest the shop's glass front. They haughtily withdrew and Ray promptly took their place, cupped his own hands and peered into the dark interior.

The layout was straightforward. Fat fryers and ovens were installed along the back wall. In front of the cooking area, glass-fronted hotplates stretched from the right-hand side. These gave way to a small, open serving area and an old till, with an entrance hatch adjacent to the left wall.

Behind the hotplates the outline of a man was visible in the gloom, apparently bent over one of the appliances. A voice in Ray's ear made him jump.

'He's been like that for hours,' said the voice. 'And all in the dark as well, what's he doing?' She sounded indignant. He turned to see an elderly lady standing alongside him, wearing a white dress with a blue, floral print. Her left hand was clasped around the handle of a two-wheeled shopping cart, which was also white, but with a red floral print. Evidently, flowers were a popular theme with her.

Ray ignored the woman, returning to the man who had reported the incident. Retrieving the notebook from his pocket, he extracted the pen from its spine and proceeded to take some details. 'What's your name, Sir?'

'Charlie Turner. I live down the road 'ere, number fifty-six.' The accent was more East End than south coast.

'Great,' said Ray. 'Can you stay here for a few minutes please, uniform will need to take a statement?'

'No probs,' said Charlie. 'You going in then?'

'I am,' said Ray, silently thanking someone up above for a helpful member of the public. He turned and addressed the growing crowd. 'Stand back please and well away from the door.' He turned back to Charlie. 'Is there a back way in, do you know?'

'Yes mate, there's a little car-park behind the shops, for the residents, like.' Charlie pointed discreetly above the shops, where a single storey ran over the parade. 'Ain't the same people what run the shops down 'ere, though. Different landlord, see?'

'I see,' said Ray. 'But there's a backyard?'

'Yes mate,' Charlie replied, cheerfully. 'Just for the bins though really, like. You go down that alley,' he pointed to the left of the parade, 'and his place is under the fire escape, well, round and about. Stinks of fish most of the time, so I'm sure you'll find it all right!'

Ray thanked him briefly and set off down the alleyway, his nose guiding him to a gate set into a brown, panelled fence. It was closed but unlocked.

Entering the small yard, Ray was surprised to see white, vertical burglar bars across the windows and an extremely solid looking door on the right-hand side, which appeared to have been further reinforced with an additional layer of plywood. The door was fitted with a latch of some description as well as two brass, mortice deadlocks, top and bottom. He stood to the far left of the concrete backyard and tried to look inside, but the bars and the light reflection on the window made it difficult to see anything. He could make out the latch and it looked expensive, a night latch possibly, the type that includes a lockable handle but contains, in addition to the automatic locking system, a bolt that projects twenty millimetres into a heavy-duty staple.

No sign of forced entry. No possible way he could force an entry either. Ray had once tried, as a Constable, to kick in a similar looking door, macho style. He had hurt his foot and ended up looking very silly; a fact the crowd of onlookers, mainly kids from the local estate, had told him in no uncertain terms at the time. A door like this, he had learnt that day, needed a battering ram.

Returning to the front of the building, he briefly considered his options. Uniform would arrive within minutes and undoubtedly look to force an immediate entry as this was a 'three one one', Tarnside police code for a suspected homicide. That the figure had been standing there for hours was insufficient reason to stop them piling in, particularly as Ray had failed to even get the woman's name to testify to this effect and she had now disappeared. He wondered briefly how she could possibly have known that. Reflecting that nobody would wait until a battering ram could be brought down to force entry round the back, Ray decided that he may as well get on with it.

Without warning, he hoofed his foot against the front door frame, praying the glass would not smash and contaminate the scene. The doorframe splintered slightly and he tried again, the small crowd drawing back with exclamations of shock and surprise. In the distance, Ray heard the wailing of a siren and this further encouraged him, a final well-placed foot on the wood saw the door bust open, the glass remained intact and he was in.

Ray took three brisk steps into the fish and chip shop and stood for a moment, sniffing the air. A sweet, sickly smell hung heavily in the stillness; a vague smell of burning mixed up with faeces and urine. The malodour of death burnt his nostrils and filled his airways. Bracing himself to duck under the hatch, he turned briefly to see heads craning in the entrance. He spun round, returned angrily to the doorway and glared outside, scowling furiously. The police siren was drawing rapidly closer.

Jabbing his finger at the crowd Ray bellowed, 'The next one who sticks their nose in here WILL be arrested, now STAY *OUT.*'

At that moment the squad car roared onto the scene, two male PCs jumped out, doors slammed and footsteps pounded over the pavement.

Chapter 13

Wind streamed through her hair and the spray whipped into her face. Rosie hung on tightly as the little speedboat shot up into the air, clearing another wave, before smacking back into the swell.

Back in the cellar, they had placed a hood on her face and put her in the back of another, smaller van. Hours later the van had slowed, performed a three point turn and come to a halt. Two men had opened the doors and one had removed the hood. Rosie had smelt fresh, salty air and seen sunlight for the first time in twenty-four hours. It was now early evening. The men's faces were covered, but they were no longer dressed as mercenaries. Both wore blue jeans, but with different coloured shirts, one blue and one white. The pair of them still wore leather gloves and Rosie figured that these rarely came off at all. The man in the blue shirt had politely helped her climb out of the van, by offering his hand.

She had taken it, climbed down and seen that they were at the end of a desolate track that led down to a pretty bay, narrow and rocky, the seabed composed of huge, oval shaped pebbles, averaging nearly a foot across apiece. White shirt had then walked away from them and proceeded to make a call. Within a few minutes, a little speedboat had arrived and then blue shirt had looked at her, before pointing at the boat expectantly. For the first time, she noticed this man was armed, some kind of pistol stuck in his trouser belt. Swiftly, she had removed her shoes, waded out and been assisted into the back of the boat by the man on board, who was dressed in the familiar black attire. Blue shirt followed, whereas white shirt went back to the van. Mysteriously, not a word had been uttered to her.

Positioned at the front of the little boat in the V-Shaped seat and looking ahead, Rosie was quite enjoying the ride. The incredible speed was exhilarating and it was so nice to be back out in the open air! Two huge outboard engines roared behind her and she saw they were approaching an island of some kind. Seagulls cried in the distance and gangs of cormorants were hanging out on isolated, rocky outcrops. Having grown up by the seaside, Rosie had gone through a bird watching phase in her youth and she still recognised all the birds and knew their names by heart. In truth, she still loved watching the seabirds.

As they drew nearer, the speedboat slowed down and Rosie heard the oystercatchers piping. Scanning the beach ahead, she spied them on the shingle, their long, red beaks making identification easy. As the boat slowed down to a gentle hum, a grey seal popped his head out of the water close by, before realizing his mistake and vanishing as quickly as he had appeared. Rosie looked up at the cliffs and saw the beautiful, white heads of the doe-eyed Fulmars, nestled into the rocky face on their chosen ledges. Then she had a brief epiphany. She looked behind her. Yes, it was still there.

Between the black-headed and common gulls, a distinctive, dark brown cap was visible, complete with a contrasting white throat and a white collar on its nape. A Great Shearwater was ducking and diving through the waves, searching for food. As she watched the bird gliding over the swell a large wave sprang up from the currents, colliding heavily with its flight path. The Great Shearwater did not flinch, cutting through the water effortlessly before dangling its feet into the water to brake, running across the ocean surface, grabbing something edible and resuming its flight. Rosie looked around quickly, scanning everything with wings until she saw another one, not far from the first. Satisfied, she looked back to the shingle beach they were approaching, a mixture of sand and pebbles.

Great Shearwaters are not a common sight in the UK, almost entirely confined to the western coast of Ireland, the Scottish Isles and the islands off the South-West coast of England. Rosie felt the hot sun on her arms and reflected that at no point had she been driven far enough to be in Northern Scotland and she had certainly not crossed over to Ireland. To have seen one Great Shearwater outside of these regions was always possible; it was unlikely, rare even, but not inconceivable. However, to have seen two of these birds together meant that she was almost certainly approaching the Scilly Isles.

***

At the sight of uniformed PCs running towards the scene most people went hastily on their way, largely aware that anyone considered a potential witness may be held and forced to give a statement, a process that can take considerable time.

Ray stood in the doorway, blocking access to the crime scene, as the two PCs ran over. Recognising him, the older of the two slowed down a little and Ray caught his eye, pointed to Charlie and said simply, 'Witness,' before turning to the younger Constable and barking brief orders at him to secure the scene and inform the Duty Officer, which the Constable promptly did and with an efficiency that Ray found quite satisfying. He turned around, took a deep breath, and retreated back into 'Fresh 'n' Salty' to examine the crime scene properly.

It was gloomy inside and Ray was tempted to turn on the light but he refrained, preferring to wait until forensics had brushed the switch for fingerprints. Walking gingerly, he bent down and stooped under the wooden hatch. Turning to his right, Ray leant his head towards the victim, extending his neck like a tortoise, waiting impatiently for his eyes to adjust to the gloom.

It was a man, dressed in a short sleeved, white, fryer's shirt with a chequered blue collar and a matching hat. Looking down, Ray could dimly make out the same chequered patterning on the trousers and a pair of casual trainers. The man was standing with his feet evenly spaced apart, bent at the waist, his head resting on the back wall. Ray took another step and gradually drew closer, leaning in further, until his face was just a foot from the dead man. He gulped and heard himself breathing as he peered, closely, at the victim's features.

The expression was terrible. In the darkness the face appeared elongated, jaw stretched, eyes wide open, mouth now locked in a permanent scream. Agonising, excruciating pain was etched into every line and feature. The eyeballs were completely rolled back and glazed whites filled the sockets.

Ray drew back, abruptly, from the ghoulish figure. He found himself perspiring and ran a hand through his hair. Then fear welled up inside him, combined with an irrational sense of panic. He swiftly quelled the emotion, stifling it, crushing it, dismissing it.

Remembering his phone was in his pocket, he fumbled for it, flicking the touchscreen which promptly emitted a cool, blue glow.

He swallowed and proceeded with his examination, kneeling down and inspecting the floor around the immobile pair of trainers. The floor looked clean in the half-light; there was no blood visible here. He could hear Frank's voice ringing in his head, '*Cause of death, Sergeant? Come on man, get on with it!*'

Shaking his head, he ruminated the possibilities. Asphyxiation, perhaps? But who would strangle a man and then take the time to try and stand him up, leaning against a wall? If that was even possible?

Holding his phone and rising slowly upright, Ray glanced down and felt a wave of cold prickles wash over his shoulders. He gasped, clutching his stomach with one hand, the other covering his mouth as he fought off a retching, lurching sensation in his guts.

His phone light revealed what had been hidden in the darkness. The man was up to his wrists in a rancid, viscous, fetid solution. Indeterminable matter was held in suspension; marrow, bone, tissue, muscle, all swilling around in a putrid, scarlet soup. A filthy scum lay over the surface.

There was no mistaking what had happened here. The victim was up to his wrists in the fat fryer.

Chapter 14

Ian Grant took a tennis ball out of his pocket and threw it up against the third floor window. The window opened and a face looked down on him. Moments later, a different tennis ball hit the pavement and Ian caught it after the first bounce. He opened the slit in the ball, retrieved the key and unlocked the door, locking it behind him. Puffing his way up the wooden flight of stairs, he arrived at the third floor and entered through an open door into a large room. Sofas and comfy armchairs were set about, some record decks and a mixer were in one corner and various speakers had been wired up around the walls. The floor was bare and painted black to match the walls. Along the left wall was a makeshift bar.

'Close the door, init.'

Ian closed the heavy, wooden door and sat down in an armchair. He tossed the tennis ball containing the key to the man, who caught it, neatly.

'All right?' said Ian.

'All right bruv. What you after?'

'Like, I was thinking of opening up shop again, you know.'

'Is it?'

'Yeah.'

There was a pause. The man blew a smoke ring. 'Nah bruv, last time you got yourself pinched, init. And you lost Tone's gun.'

'I said you could leave it at mine, not dat I wanted it. Not my fault the feds busted me that same day. Maybe whoever dropped it off was being followed, you get me?'

Another pause.

'I see you talking to the feds the other day.'

Ian gulped. 'Yeah man, they was asking questions and that, but I din't have nothing to say.'

'What's they asking?'

'Just asking if there was any new faces around, like foreigners, on the manor. I said nah, I ain't seen no-one like that.'

'Is it?'

'Yeah. But he said he weren't looking at nothing else. Not right now, he says.'

'Hmm.' The man paused and blew another smoke ring. 'I ain't setting you up right now. Wait until the feds have got off your case. Then, we'll see.'

'All right man, it's cool. I'll just score a henry for now, man, percy.'

'Cool bro. Proper sticky, funky skunk in right now. It's twenty-fives though bruv, if you just want one.'

***

'Close the road off completely, residents only,' Frank was directing the Duty Officer, 'and close off the other side of the pavement before the press get here, I want them kept well out of our way. Extend that cordon.'

'Guv,' confirmed Inspector Alfred Robertson.

'And find out who owns these vehicles and get them moved, ASAP.'

'I'll get someone on it, guv,' said Alfred, nodding his agreement, before turning away and walking smartly to one of the PCs by the police tape.

'Where the hell is Jackson?'

'Right here, guv,' Ray replied.

'Oh, there you are,' said Frank, turning around to face him. 'You first on scene?'

'Yes guv.'

Frank nodded. 'Good,' he said, rather to Ray's surprise.

He started walking, motioning over his shoulder to Ray to follow. White screens now blocked the windows and police tape enclosed the small expanse of grass and pavement that stretched out in front of the parade. Behind the tape, a throng of uniformed and plain-clothed officers parted as Frank bowled his way through them, the old prop forward pushing his way through the field.

'Are you done?' he said to James, the police photographer, who was looking rather pale. James shook his head. Frank paused, turning to his right. 'Who are you?' The cameraman placed a lit cigarette back in his mouth and fumbled for his credentials, before holding them up. 'Good man, well done. Off you go now, it's getting rather cramped round here.' Stopping outside the white screens, Frank wiped his brow with a white handkerchief, before he turned to face Ray and spoke more quietly. 'Right, run me through events. And I want to know *exactly* who has been in that building.'

Ray had followed procedure to the letter, initially allowing nobody to enter the crime scene until the divisional surgeon had arrived and declared life extinct. Insisting both men had donned full protective clothing, Ray had then allowed access to the police photographer, assisting him to set up a single light on the shop floor with instructions to stay well back from the victim, before the cameraman had been allowed inside to film the obligatory crime scene video.

Whilst the recording and initial photographs of the crime scene were being shot, five additional PCs had arrived in a further two squad cars, followed shortly afterwards by an unmarked vehicle containing the Detective Chief Inspector and Detective Constable Jason Stephenson. The forensics van had then pulled up and been forced to park at right angles, behind one of the squad cars and tight to a garden wall. Although unintentional, this had the benefit of completely blocking pedestrian access from the south side. Three men in white garb now moved slowly inside the building, the interior lighting causing grossly misshapen silhouettes to be projected onto the white screening.

'Oompa Loompas,' said Jason in Ray's ear, nodding at the silhouettes. 'Imported direct from Loompa Land.'

Ray smiled for the first time since he had emerged from the horrendous sight inside. He spun about, placed his hands on his hips and bent at the waist. Leaning forward and waggling a finger at Jason, he sang at him, '*I don't like the look of it.*'

'Jackson!' He turned to see a purple-faced Frank stood behind him. 'Stop fucking about! The Press are over there!'

Ray looked over and noticed the press photographers for the first time, their cameras rattling off shots like machine gun fire at the edge of the cordoned area. 'Sorry guv.'

'Will you ever grow up?'

When Ray glanced back, Jason had vanished. A moment later Ray caught sight of him again, now some distance behind Frank, holding his nose, shoulders shaking. Ray opened his mouth to reply, but could think of nothing to say, so closed it again.

'Paul Harding is taking the lead on this case,' Frank continued. 'I trust you can work with one of our own Detective Superintendents without causing me any more grief?'

Ray nodded. Frank leant into him. 'Say it please, Detective Sergeant.'

'No problem guv. I mean…I will look forward to working under DSI Harding, guv.'

'Good.' Frank stood back. 'Well done on securing the scene, an excellent job. Using the White Light, forensics have already picked up the footprints of three, separate men, apparently stood around the victim at the time of death.'

Ray beamed a smile of genuine, professional satisfaction. 'Excellent,' he said, which made Frank smile in turn.

'Good work, Sergeant. Paul has asked me to appoint him a Deputy SIO, who will be required to take an active lead in this enquiry.'

Frank stepped back from Ray and took a moment to look at him. Ray held his breath. Frank seemed to have a twinkle in his eye.

'Welcome to your first proper homicide investigation as the Deputy Senior Investigating Officer, DS Jackson. Now, don't let me down.'

Chapter 15

Rosie knew nothing about the layout of the island as, shortly after spotting the Great Shearwater, the familiar, blackout hood had been thrown in her direction by blue shirt, who had then waved his gun at it. Frightened, she had obliged, placing it over her head and pulling the cord around her neck, her world once more plunged into stifling darkness. The boat had then speeded up again, done a few turns on the spot and driven on for some distance, before finally pulling up.

Now imprisoned and looking out across the ocean, Rosie began to wonder if she would ever get home. Despite, apparently, being on an island she was not free to wander around, confined instead to a suite on the third floor that constituted part of an elegant mansion. The path of the sun had revealed that her suite was facing roughly south, the view stretching out across an apparently endless ocean.

The garden in front of her was beautiful, the beds packed with a variety of blooming bushes and flowers, entirely surrounded by a very high, redbrick wall. A flat, well-tended formal lawn led to an ornamental, cream wall composed of elegant, concrete balustrades. Giant urns marked the entrance to centred, sweeping steps that opened out onto a lower lawn, which ran down invitingly to a private, sandy beach.

Her quarters were not luxurious but they were comfortable, comprising a bathroom situated behind a double bedroom, in front of which stood a large sitting room. Folding double doors partitioned the sitting room from the bedroom, so it was, effectively, one large room. Rosie had found a few different changes of clothes on the bed and some basic toiletries in the bathroom. A roll-on deodorant, a toothbrush, toothpaste, shampoo, conditioner, soap and a nail file block; nothing metal of any description. Looking through the bedroom window, Rosie reasoned that the back of the bathroom must face due east and was, most likely, an exterior wall.

Still hooded upon arrival, Rosie had counted garden steps and paces and done her utmost to remember every twist and turn inside, before entering her quarters and realizing that it had been a rather futile exercise. She could see from her window where they had pulled up on the beach, right below her. She could see she was on the third floor. Her heart sank. The number of turns and stairs she had counted between here and the garden felt of little relevance now. She was completely trapped and nobody was ever going to find her.

***

It was late when Ray arrived at the hospital. He knew from experience that toxicology admissions were initially taken to the Assessment Suite. From there, patients were normally transferred to Ward Twenty, where the nursing staff have additional training and experience in the care of patients with poisoning and deliberate self-harm issues. Ray went straight to Ward Twenty and walked briskly through the corridors, hoping he could find the patient before he was approached by a member of the hospital staff. PC Greene had given him a fairly detailed description and Ray felt confident he would know the woman when he saw her.

Unobtrusively, Ray slipped through the corridors, poking his head surreptitiously through numerous disposable curtains pulled hastily around trolley beds. It was very quiet on the ward and the lights had been turned down a notch. Disinfectant and illness combined to hang heavily in the sterile, breathless atmosphere. As he passed by, a low moaning sound began from one of the beds behind him. Ray shuddered and moved on swiftly. He hated hospitals.

Eventually, he found his way to a patient matching the description. The girl was fast asleep. She had flaxen hair but it was filthy. It looked like she had tried to plait it into dreadlocks in one area on the right of her head, but it was now a tangled, matted mess.
He slipped in behind the curtain and checked the observation chart at the end of her bed. TOX was written in red pen and circled at the top of the sheet; Ray knew this was short for 'toxicology patient'. He glanced at the name box. It just read, 'Ellie'.

Replacing the observation sheet, Ray walked round to her bedside. She looked younger than he had expected, maybe sixteen or seventeen. Her face was pale and an intravenous drip was plugged into her right arm. Ellie lay on her left side in a white gown, testament to the fact they had stripped her top half to perform an ECG, probably in the ambulance. Her face was streaked with grime and Ray realized she had been crying. Her pillow was dirty now. A burst of anger exploded inside him, quite unexpectedly, as he wondered why nobody had even bothered to wash her face. Just rammed a drip in her arm, transferred her from the AS to Ward Twenty and left her here. Somebody else's problem now.

He sighed heavily. What the hell was she doing running around the streets? Not for the first time, Ray wondered why nobody seemed to care. How it was still possible that kids like this just fell through the cracks of the system. Staring at her young, pretty, oval face, Ray felt overwhelmed by sadness. He sat down heavily in an armchair next to the bed, sinking into the thick, foam cushions. His last thought was that he was probably over-tired and a bit overwrought. It had been a long day.

Chapter 16

The briefing room was packed. An enormous screen filled most of the rear wall and alongside this another square screen was also infixed, the latter used primarily for projections and presentations. Officers of all ranks filled the available space, sitting in chairs and on desks and many more standing, all faces staring grimly at the Detective Chief Inspector.

'Our Police Search Advisor is Detective Sergeant Emma Drake and she is now assigned to this taskforce. Detective Inspector Norman Beattie is the Inquiries Officer and, in this case, he should be the main point of contact for you all. Detective Superintendent Paul Harding is overseeing as Deputy SIO, whilst Detective Chief Superintendent Manson will be taking the lead as SIO. Some of you may find your workloads increased until this crisis has been resolved. I don't need to remind you that time is of the essence here. This is being treated as a 'High Risk' incident and involves a high-ranking officer. I am not willing to go into the details of Rosie's current investigations, but obviously this is something Norman, Paul and I will be discussing in more detail. For now, I want every informant, every possible contact and lead you gentlemen, and ladies, have at your disposal, thoroughly wrung out. Norman?'

Detective Inspector Norman Beattie stood up and came to the front of the room. He was a stocky man, barrel chested and clean shaven, with arms like an ape on steroids. He was also Ray's line manager, although Ray barely spoke to him from one month to the next, both parties happy to operate with the minimum of compulsory interaction. 'I don't really need to point this out,' Norman began, 'but just remember we are ALL on this taskforce as members of this station.' He took a moment to survey the grim faces that looked up at him, before continuing.

'This is a meeting none of us ever wished to have. In the appropriate timeframe, more external troops may well be assigned to the taskforce to help us out. In the meantime, expect to put in some long days and be willing to step up and take on more responsibility where you can.' He stopped, noticing a movement at the back of the room. He stood back and to one side. The Detective Chief Superintendent, Albert Manson, came forward from where he had been quietly standing at the back of the room. He turned and faced the assembled officers.

'I know some of you may think this an over-reaction after you return to your desks,' Alfred stated. He had a mild manner about him, a fact that had frequently led people to under-estimate his capabilities, which included a ruthless efficiency and a merciless approach to criminality. His lack of empathy had once caused Frank to confide to his wife, Anna, that he believed the man to be bordering on the psychopathic. This had stuck with Anna, who remained unclear as to whether Frank had been joking. He had not.

'However,' Albert continued, 'I can assure you that prior to her recent promotion we undertook extensive psychological profiling at my specific request. Competition was fierce for the vacant DI position and I wanted to be absolutely certain that we promoted the best person into that role. I believe we did.

'The point here is that the tests confirmed our own beliefs and understanding regarding how DI Blake operates, thinks, reacts and interacts. I *can* reveal to you that she is a highly intelligent individual, highly intelligent. Barring some sort of unprecedented break from character or unforeseen eventuality which nobody here has successfully been able to imagine or envisage, assume this is either an abduction, or a murder enquiry.

'Take care out there. That is all.'

***

When Ellie opened her eyes, the first thing she saw was a man asleep in the chair next to her bedside. The curtains around her bed were pulled back and sunlight was streaming in through the windows.

Ellie frowned, puzzled, then her countenance cleared. The man must be with another patient. Maybe this was the only seat free and he had slipped into it and dropped off. She turned onto her back and lay there for a few minutes, staring at the ceiling, before realizing she needed to pee. Unsure quite what to do with the drip in her arm, she made an effort to sit up. The man remained asleep.

Ellie called over quietly to a nurse at a neighbouring patient's bedside, who helped her to get up and go to the toilet. When she returned and got back into bed, the man was still there. She watched him while she rested, pretending that he was there for her. He was quite good looking, probably late twenties, a few days of stubble, short, cropped, mousy brown hair. He had a terrible taste in shirts though, that collar was seriously dated. As she stared, he opened his eyes and immediately she looked away.

'Oh my God,' Ray exclaimed. 'Shit!'

There was a moment's pause.

'Morning,' she replied, turning to look at him again. 'Sleep well?'

He stared at her, blinking, for a moment. Then her heart skipped a beat.

'Ellie!' said Ray.

Chapter 17

Rosie had no idea how to escape her makeshift prison, but she determined that there had to be a way.

The old windows had been enclosed by burglar bars, cemented into the brickwork, retaining the aesthetics of the building but meaning that now they could only be opened a crack. Escaping through a window, she conceded after a few minutes of examining them, was impossible.

Rosie lay back on the bed and wracked her brains, but nothing sprung to mind. Further examination revealed the carpet was firmly fixed in place, glued down presumably, before having been fastened to the grippers. In addition, a gold trim was tightly screwed down around the entire circumference, running tight along the wall's edge in every direction. Sighing heavily, she glumly admitted to herself that even if she did manage to lift some part of it, she had absolutely no way of hacking through floorboards or prising them up, let alone breaking through the ceiling below and swinging down to freedom on a bed sheet.

She considered the sitting room door. She had visions of breaking it down, overcoming her armed guard and then fighting her way to freedom. The idea was at best fanciful, at worst, ludicrous.

Oh think, think. What would Bond do?

She was a big fan of James Bond, particularly the new model whom she considered rather dishy. Bond would escape through a secret tunnel...or laser through the window bars with his special watch.

Why don't I have a special watch?

Cursing aloud, she went into the bathroom and ran herself a deep, hot bath. Climbing in, she lay back and stared at the ceiling. She closed her eyes, trying to relax, but the small fan in the ceiling hummed noisily, further irritating her.

Suddenly, she opened her eyes, wide open, and looked up at the ceiling. The small fan continued whirring away overhead. Small spotlights had been infixed and they beamed down on her as she tried desperately to bring back memories from her childhood.

A hideous pink toilet, enormous mirrors, a gold-trimmed Jacuzzi, pink carpets, white cupboards with gold handles. Her father up a ladder, her mother taking her away by the hand, plaster, horsehair, lathe, dustsheets…she remembered her father telling her what he was doing. 'It's the plaster, Rosie. The damp has made it all rotten but don't worry, soon we will have a nice, new, shiny bathroom.' She remembered his smile and closed her eyes again. Cancer was a savage bastard.

What did she know about plaster? And where did the lathe come into it?

Oh think! You know this!

Plaster was laid on top of mortar. It was the mortar that was spread over the lathe. The lathe was laid across the joists, thin strips of it, up in the loft!

The fan above her must be taking the steam and humidity straight up and out, via an overhead attic. And the plaster in the old bathrooms always went soft, her builder had told her that recently when she had built her new en suite. 'You don't want none of that plaster or drywall, love. UVPC panels and a proper sealant. And we'll put the fan out the exterior wall.'

Rosie smiled. She remembered the conversation quite clearly now.

So, if she could just remove that fan from the ceiling…

***

Ellie blinked big, blue eyes at Ray from the hospital bed.

'Hello,' she said.

Totally unprepared, Ray tried to gather himself, still half asleep. He retrieved his phone from his pocket, pulling it out just as the nurse came over. 'No phones in here please, it interferes with the equipment.' She watched over Ray until he put it back in his pocket, then turned to Ellie. 'Feeling better?'

Ellie nodded. 'Yes thank you.'

'Good, we'll have that drip out of you today and you can be on your way,' said the nurse, smiling down at her. Without breaking eye contact with Ellie, the nurse nodded in Ray's direction and added brightly, 'Your friend has been here all night.'

Ray ran his fingers through his hair. Ellie was smiling but not looking at him.

'Hello Ellie,' he began. He was about to run through his usual spiel but he forgot it for some reason. He turned to the nurse. 'Can we get her a wash, please? Maybe a bath?'

'This isn't a hotel I'm afraid. You'll have to let her have one at your own expense. Won't be long now, though.' She beamed at Ellie again, before wheeling off a metal trolley stacked with dangerous-looking, red pills.

Ellie was still smiling at the ceiling.

'I'm Ray,' he began, awkwardly.

She turned and fixed her eyes on his. 'Thank you for staying with me.'

'Oh. Right. Yes.'

Before he could gather his thoughts, Ellie asked him, 'Are you a police officer?'

'Yes, that's right,' he replied, somewhat relieved that she had worked that out. 'I just popped in last night, but you were asleep here.'

'Yes, I'm in hospital.'

'Well…yes…quite,' Ray finished lamely. He wondered what the hell was wrong with him. He cleared his throat and sat up straight. He had to break eye contact for a moment. He found her eyes quite hypnotic.

'I can answer some questions if you like,' she said, returning her gaze to the ceiling, smiling.

'Where are you going to stay?' Ray blurted out, immediately wondering what on earth had possessed him to ask such a personal question. Why had he asked her that? Now she was looking at him again.

'That's a funny question,' she said without blinking.

'Oh no, not really,' said Ray, breezily. 'Just in case I need to get hold of you again. For something or other. You know, follow up on enquiries, that sort of thing.' Shifting slightly in his seat, Ray retrieved a crumpled notebook from his back pocket and made a point of writing something down.

'Uh huh,' she said. 'Well, I'm not sure just at the moment.'

Ray put his pad down. This was awful. 'I came to take a statement from you, find out where you scored the gear. That's why I came here,' he admitted.

'I know,' Ellie replied, turning to smile at the ceiling again. A brief silence followed, before she continued, 'Tell you what, I'll do you a deal. You find me somewhere to stay tonight and, if I like it, I'll tell you what you want to know. Deal?'

'Deal,' said Ray.

Chapter 18

Having slept for a solid thirteen hours at the hospital, Ray had completely missed the compulsory meeting about the missing Rosie Blake. Picking up the message on his phone, he had promptly raced back to the station from the hospital, arriving just as the meeting had broken up. Jason had swiftly briefed him, before Frank had appeared and called him into his office. Unaware that Ray had only just arrived at the station, Frank looked tired and stressed as he thanked him for his recent assistance.

'I want DI Beattie to devote all of his time to finding Rosie Blake so, until that is resolved, you will report to directly to me. Mark also has enough on his plate. Unofficially, so do I.'

Frank exhaled loudly, before continuing. 'With regards to the fryer victim, John Harrington, you will have to make most of the running. Detective Superintendent Harding is on the Blake case and overseeing a larger team on that front, but he remains the SIO on your murder enquiry, for now. So he is effectively heading up two Incident Rooms at the moment and is likely to be under enormous pressure. Make sure you report to him without fail. I'm sure you know his reputation by now.'

Detective Superintendent Paul Harding was a fearsome character. He was tall and lean, with short cropped, blond hair. Paul thought that was what had given rise to his nickname, 'Blondie', but this was, in fact, attributable to his steely blue eyes. His eyes seemed to exist half-closed, in a perpetual squint, in a manner strongly reminiscent of Clint Eastwood's character in 'The Good, The Bad and The Ugly'. It was also rumoured that he had spent almost a year so deep undercover that the brass had begun to wonder whose side he was really on.

Frank drew back a little and opened a file on his desk. 'How's the new boy?' he enquired, shuffling through some paperwork.

'He's very good guv.'

'Very good, eh?' Frank looked up, allowing his countenance to relax a little. 'That's a rare compliment from you DS Jackson.'

'Is it? Well, so far he's been very thorough. Punctual, organised.'

'He was also in here singing your praises earlier. I do hope this isn't some kind of conspiracy?'

'Conspiracy, guv?'

Frank spoke gently, 'Yes, conspiracy, you know what that means DS Jackson.' He scrutinised the face of his Detective Sergeant for a few seconds. 'Well, I am glad you two seem to be getting along. It does make for a better working environment when people aren't rubbing one another up the wrong way, don't you find?'

'Oh yes, guv. Absolutely. He seems very keen to learn.'

'How refreshing,' Frank replied, cutely. He took a moment before continuing. 'There are two further DCs assigned to your taskforce to assist with the murder enquiry, Mitchell Wright and Rachel Allcorn. They work well together and should be able to carry out orders without any handholding. I suggest you keep working with Jason Stephenson as a pair for now, that seems to be working well and he's inexperienced. I'm afraid that's all I can spare just at the moment. Your Incident Room is being managed by DS Galford, I think you've worked with Robert before?'

Ray nodded. 'Yes, guv.'

'Good. He's an experienced Office Manager and you're lucky to have him. He can fill you in on the admin side of things, but it's a skeleton crew as you would expect at the moment. Well, that is all for now, thank you.' Ray stood to leave and Frank looked up at him. 'Ray?'

'Guv?'

'One other thing. You may not be on Rosie's taskforce but you have a few ears to the ground. Do your best, won't you?'

Ray looked down at the Detective Chief Inspector. There was no humour in Frank's eyes now, just grim concern written into his face. Ray replied softly.

'I'll do that, guv.'

Frank paused and looked at Ray. 'You remember the case you worked a few years ago, the opium den in Brook Hill?'

Ray nodded, waiting for him to continue. 'Good. And you remember what was being pushed around?' said Frank, motioning for him to sit back down.

'Black and Brown, usual stuff,' Ray replied, resuming his seat.

'Elaborate.'

'Well, they are both H3 grade, although the Black Tar is often referred to as 'three point five', or 'three and a half'. On our ground, it was being sold as 'three star'. Black tar is actually an acetate salt, suitable for injection "as is" when properly prepared. As it benefits from the addition of a small amount of something acidic, a very small amount of lemon juice is most commonly used. It is sometimes smoked, but usually the 'three star' was generally bought by the needle junkies, for injection.' Ray paused before continuing.

'Brown is an acetylated base. It is smokable "as is" and it's usually what the first timers take. To be suitable for injection it needs to be prepared, again most commonly with citric acid.'

Frank nodded. 'What am I am about to share goes no further. DI Blake was working on a very important investigation, in conjunction with SOCA. In short, we already knew about the H4 found in the warehouse, but it's relatively new on our ground and we don't know who is supplying it.'

'Is it China White?'

'The same stuff, but most likely coming in from Afghanistan. And it's not a Fentanyl derivative either, Rosie got hold of some and we've had it analysed. Seventy-six percent pure grade heroin. Then she disappeared.' Frank put his hand to his forehead and closed his eyes for a second. Opening them, he leant forward, crossing his hands over his desk.

'Therefore, with regards to the OD in the warehouse, the more you can take care of on your own, the better. Hopefully we can get a swift ID off forensics. It's the second body in as many weeks and it looks likely there are going to be more of them. You understand?'

Ray nodded, before Frank continued. 'I cannot stress the importance of this enough. I need these bastards stopped. You do understand me, Ray? I need a result before more people die.'

Chapter 19

Knowing very little about homelessness, Ray did not immediately understand the implications of the deal he had struck with Ellie. However, within an hour or so he was beginning to find out.

Obtaining emergency accommodation from the council at short notice required the person to present as 'Vulnerable' or 'Priority Need'. Once Ray had established Ellie was nineteen, not pregnant, had no local connections, had not previously been in care, had no criminal record or convictions, no history of violence, presented as the lowest risk, according to the Liaison Psychiatry Service at the hospital, with no mental health issues or history of self harm and was classed as a recreational drug user with no obvious dependency issues — Ray was beginning to understand the reality of the situation.

He eventually called the Tarnside council 'Homelessness Unit' and spoke to a woman who advised him, in nasal tones, that the young woman in question would probably be able to find a bed at the local YMCA, but that she would have to pay for it.

'In common with all emergency housing these days, I'm afraid. But that's the Conservatives for you, isn't it?' she drawled. 'Cut, cut, cut and who picks up the pieces, hmm? The 'Big Society'?'

Ray hung up.

Stumped, he called his two additional Detective Constables and asked them how their house-to-house enquiries were getting on in Clifton Street. Nothing to report. Apparently nobody had seen anything. Ray encouraged them to keep pushing for answers, somebody must have seen something. There was no CCTV directly on the Clifton Street shopping parade anymore; there had been once, but the local kids had kept using the camera for target practice and one them was a mean shot with an air rifle. However, forensics had confirmed that the victim had died late the previous evening, between ten and eleven, which coincided with the obvious assumption that at least three men had gone into 'Fresh 'n' Salty' around closing time, the previous day. If the men had been walking in the vicinity towards the scene together, then it was likely they could spot and potentially identify the group. If they had arrived at the scene separately or from different directions, then it would be a lot more difficult. Ray left instructions with Jason to go through all the CCTV recordings of the surrounding streets and see what he could uncover.

Ray finally left the station and drove to the hospital, unsure of what he would say when he got there and increasingly concerned that Ellie would have simply vanished back into the ether by the time he arrived.

To his relief, Ellie was still in her bed, but the drip had been removed and she was having something to eat. She saw him walking down the corridor, finished her mouthful and started to smile. As Ray walked up to her bedside, he saw her smiling, her chin down on her chest, apparently looking down at the tray in front of her. Unaware he had been spotted, Ray greeted her cheerfully as he walked over.

'Is that nice?' he said, motioning to the tray in front of her.

Ellie looked up at him and fixed big, blue eyes on his. Once again, Ray found himself slightly flustered and taken aback. She did have a penetrating stare. He blinked. She held his gaze.

'Hello,' she said.

'Hi,' Ray replied, much more quietly. He sat down in the armchair. It was extremely comfortable, he reflected.

'It's very nice, thank you.'

'Oh. Right. Good.'

She smiled at him. 'How are you?'

The question completely threw him again. Nobody had asked Ray *how* he was feeling for...well, actually Ray could not remember. He sat there for a moment with his mouth open, before quickly replying, 'Fine, fine. Yes, I'm fine. How are you, more to the point?'

Ellie finished her meal and turned to him. 'Much better now,' she smiled. As he watched, the smile faded from her face. She sat back and looked back at the ceiling. Misery clouded her countenance. 'The nurse says I can leave today.'

This was all new territory for Ray. He had never seen anybody *sad* to be leaving hospital before, especially with a clean bill of health. The harsh reality of her situation crept down his spine like an ice cube. In an effort to hide his empathy, Ray smiled, bravely.

Suddenly, Ellie brightened up. She looked at him again, big eyes wide open. 'Have you found me somewhere to stay?'

Ray's heart jumped into his throat. He opened his mouth and closed it again. He was used to dealing with criminals, pushing heads into walls, chasing down robbers, tracking down villains, these were things he knew how to do, how to feel about.

'It's okay,' she said, closing her eyes and lying back against the pillow. 'I know.'

Ray had never felt so helpless. Silence.

'The YMCA, right?' she asked him, as he struggled to compose a response. He exhaled heavily.

'That's what they told me, yeah. I did try hard. I…' He broke off. For the first time he understood what the expression meant: sick to the stomach. He looked at the floor, absent-mindedly chewing his lip.

'I don't want to go there,' she said, quietly. 'It's just one big dormitory full of bunk beds. Hundreds of them. But don't worry. I know a few places I can go.'

He looked up at her and noticed she was looking at him. Her face was soft, the eyes full of compassion. 'It's okay,' she said, gently.

This was intense. And all the wrong way round. He felt about twelve years old again.

'NO,' he said, too loudly.

'No?'

Ray shook his head. 'No.'

***

Entering her quarters, the guard placed the tray on the coffee table in the sitting room. 'Enjoy,' he said. He left the room, closing the door quietly behind him.

Rosie stared at the food suspiciously. It was the first thing anybody had said to her since her arrival on this godforsaken island. Picking up the tray, she withdrew into the bedroom, closing the partition doors. However outlandish the suggestion seemed in the cold light of day, the suspicion remained that she was being watched in the sitting room, either through an unseen aperture or by a hidden camera.

Quickly, she took her plate of food into the bathroom and scraped it into the toilet. Something about the guard this evening did not sit right with her at all. Besides, she was not taking any chances, not tonight! Barefoot, she stood on the bath and removed the square, plastic cover from around the small extractor fan – or at least where the fan used to be! Her sensible shoes had made short work of that. The heel made an effective hammer when the shoe was held by the toe end and swung with force. Already, she could easily get her arm up and inside the aperture.

She had held it there for a few minutes at first, fondly imagining a cool breeze would blow gently through her fingertips; but she could not determine anything very much, other than it was very dark, very dirty and very hot up there. The plaster and lathe was roughly six inches thick, old, damp and crumbly. Even now, she was itching to start tearing at the ceiling but still she refrained. Not long to wait now.

Chapter 20

Frank was sitting with his elbows on his desk, head in his hands. The door to his office was open, as was his custom unless he had company. At the sound of a quick knock, he looked up.

'Frank?' It was the Detective Superintendent, Paul Harding. 'You got a minute, Frank?'

'Of course.'

Paul entered, shutting the door behind him. He held out a DVD over the desk. Frank looked at him, grimly, before taking it from his outstretched hand.

'She's alive, Frank.'

Frank felt tremendous relief. It was almost tangible, as if a physical weight had been lifted from his shoulders. He sat back in his seat. 'Thank God,' he exclaimed. 'Thank the Lord!'

'It's not all good news,' Paul replied.

'Is she hurt?'

'Not as far as we can tell. But the transit van we suspect has not turned up and the trail went cold about fifteen miles west of here. The DVD is not much, it just shows her watching some television a few days ago. The bastards are filming her with some hidden camera by the looks of it. That's just a copy. I thought you might want to look at it though. We've had our guys take a look at the original but…well, to be honest she could be anywhere.'

'Thanks, Paul,' said Frank, forgetting titles in his relief. Paul let that one go without comment. 'When did you get it?'

'It came this morning, in the regular mail. Marked for the attention of the Superintendent. As soon as he saw it, he passed it straight to me.'

'I see.'

The two men held each other's stare for a moment. Frank swallowed hard. He was struggling to ask the obvious question. Paul answered it for him.

'One million pounds, Frank. Within seventy-two hours.'

Frank did not know quite what to say. He sat at his desk, nodding, absorbing the news. 'Have they left a contact number?' he asked.

'No. They sent a pay-as-you-go phone. The first call comes in forty-eight hours, well, forty-eight hours from six o'clock this evening to be precise.'

Frank wiped his nose with his fist. He looked up. 'Anything else you can tell me?'

'Nothing. The truth is Frank, there's nothing else I can say anyway. We have an incident room full of people with nothing to do. SOCA have steamed in with their Anti Kidnap & Extortion Unit, we have additional units from the Covert Policing Branch, officers and staff from the Cultural and Community Resource Unit with their database. The Firearms Unit are on standby, desperate to know when they can start shooting someone. The Met have offered a team from their Kidnap & Specialist Investigation Unit, they clearly have sod all to do either. Everyone is frantically trying to look busy up there but, in basic terms, we have absolutely no idea where she is or who's holding her. Oh, and the Assistant Chief Constable is now officially heading up the investigation, by the way.'

'Great,' said Frank, making no effort to hide his sarcasm. 'I bet Manson is friggin' thrilled about that. So, what are you now? Deputy Deputy Senior Investigating Officer?'

'Something like that, yeah,' Paul replied, allowing himself a rare smile.

'What about the van? Surely you got a trace on the plates, at least?'

'Yeah, traffic cameras got us a fix on the plates, they were from a scrap merchants, same model, same make. It's a ringer Frank, but we've had every traffic cop and camera in the country keeping an eye out, so it's obviously been dumped, burnt out or scrapped somewhere or other. Nothing has turned up though, I've had guys scouring every scrapyard…' Paul broke off. 'You get the picture.'

Frank nodded glumly. 'Thanks for filling me in, guvnor.'

Paul nodded. 'Well, I just thought you'd like to know. Let's just pray for a break.' He opened the door and turned to leave the room, leaving Frank to watch the DVD alone. As he left, Paul deliberately and gently closed the door behind him.

***

Ellie did up her seatbelt as Ray pulled out of the hospital car park. She was a quiet little thing, Ray reflected. Frequently her forehead was mildly creased, as if she was thinking hard or slightly anxious. She stared out of the passenger window. They drove in silence for a few minutes before Ray spoke first.

'You all right?'

She turned to him and smiled briefly. 'Yes. I was just thinking.'

'I saw you had your thinking face on,' he replied. He was smiling, but Ellie was staring out of the window again and did not notice.

'Do you live on your own, then?' she asked.

'Yes. I told you that already.' There was a brief silence. 'I'm not in a lot, to be honest,' Ray continued. 'Just seems silly, the house just sitting there empty. You with nowhere to go. Me with a spare room I don't use.' There was another brief silence. 'That's all,' said Ray.

'Is it?' She turned to look at him. 'That's all, is it?'

He looked straight back at her this time, without flinching. 'That's all, Ellie. I can promise you that.'

She looked straight ahead. 'You don't even know me.'

'No,' Ray said. 'I don't know you. If you want to screw me over and steal my shit and run out and buy crack with it, that's up to you. I just don't think you will. But you're right, I don't know you.'

She nodded, seemingly approving of the logic of this argument. Ray continued, 'I don't want to be laying down rules here really but erm…please, don't invite people back to my house.'

She looked shocked. 'Oh no, I wouldn't do that. Never.'

Ray smiled. 'Good, that's all right then.' He drove on down the wide, tree-lined avenue that led from the hospital to the city centre for another minute before indicating, pulling over and cutting the engine. He turned in his seat and faced her. 'Look, you don't have to do anything you don't want to do. If you want to get out and walk, that's fine. Now or anytime. You're welcome to stay at my place until you get yourself sorted, it's not a big deal. I work all the time anyway. It's up to you. Just…just don't go telling people where I live and who I am and what I do, that's all. That's all I ask. I don't know who you know. In case you're wondering, that's my main issue right now.'

Ellie weighed this up for a moment. Then she looked at him directly and spoke calmly in reply. 'I know a few people, Ray, but they're not my friends. You don't need to worry about that.' She inclined her head slightly and looked across at him, questioningly. 'Okay?'

'Okay,' he said. Ray realized that she seemed to have taken complete control of the conversation. There was a pause before he added, 'Are you okay?'

She nodded. 'I'm good. Better now I know what you were thinking.'

Chapter 21

The sky was overcast as Ray pulled up in front of his modest, end of terrace, two up, two down home. It was a quiet street in the Pebble Hill district, set back on a street that lay a few hundred yards from the sea. Switching off the engine, he saw Ellie beaming. 'This is nice,' she said.

It was Ray's first house and he was quite proud of it. He suddenly realized that she was the first person he had ever brought back here, despite moving in over a year ago. 'Thanks,' he said, modestly.

His mobile phone rang and it was Jason, updating him on the CCTV footage. 'I think I might have something guv,' he said, excitedly. Ray congratulated him and told him to keep at it. 'I'm not going to be back in today,' Ray added. 'Go home yourself soon, get something to eat and some sleep. Nobody works well when they are really tired. And that's not an excuse to go out on the piss, either,' he added.

Hanging up, he saw Ellie watching. 'So, do people report to you, then?'

'Yeah. Only a few though.'

'Wow,' she said, impressed. 'So, what's your job again?'

'I'm a Sergeant. But really, that's only one above a Constable. There's uniform and CID, right? So in CID you just stick 'detective' in front of the rank. So I'm a Detective Sergeant now.'

'Cool,' she said, before adding, 'Shall we get out?'

'Yep.'

Ray knew he should ring his other DCs, but he just did not want to right now. It could wait until the morning, in fact it all could. It had occurred to Ray when he was pulling up that he had barely seen a soul outside of work for the past twelve months. He was certainly not going back to work this evening, he actually had a guest for once. He led the way into his home, which was clean and tidy, albeit sparsely furnished. The downstairs was open plan with an electric fireplace. Upstairs were two double bedrooms, both roughly the same size, and a bathroom.

Ray showed Ellie his tiny kitchen and got her a cold drink, before inviting her to sit on the couch and watch television while he sorted the spare room. Then he thought better of it and told her to go and have a bath 'or something' he added, not wishing to offend her.

'Thanks,' she replied. 'Can I borrow a razor?' At which point Ray had shown her up to the bathroom, left her some razors, jokingly pointing out it was a good job that he preferred disposables, and gone to find her some spare clothes. 'I don't really have much that's going to fit,' Ray said, scratching his head. 'But I'll leave you something outside the door.' He managed to dig out some boxer shorts that he never worn as they were far too tight, some old, elasticated tracksuit bottoms and a clean shirt.

By the time she had showered, Ray had moved various boxes around his spare room, made up a bed on the air mattress he had once bought but never used and started cooking some bolognaise downstairs. Ellie came downstairs and curled up on his couch as if she had been living there for months. From her seat, she could see directly through to the kitchen where Ray was standing, preparing the dinner. Behind her, the television was on mute and churning out endless news stories.

'All right?' he said.

'Thanks, that was a really good shower!'

'Hungry?'

'Starving.'

Glancing up, he noticed that she looked a lot older now, all of a sudden. How strange, he thought. Amazing what a wash and a change of clothes can do.

'So,' she said, 'Why no girlfriend? Are you gay?'

Ray smiled broadly. 'Not gay,' he replied. 'I think you would know if I was. I thought women picked up on these things?'

Ellie winked at him. 'Never know,' she said.

Still smiling, Ray kept opening the tinned plum tomatoes and then started boiling the kettle for the pasta.

'So?' she prompted.

'Very direct, aren't you?' Ray asked, trying in vain to contain his amusement.

'Just curious,' she replied.

Ray's countenance changed, a flash of sadness crossing his face. He turned away briefly to stir the mince on the hob, out of sight. He swiftly re-appeared, pushing memories from his mind. Things he never dwelt on anymore.

'No, not seeing anyone at the moment,' he said, airily. There was a silence.

'Sorry,' she said.

'Eh? Oh no, don't be silly. It's a fair cop,' he punned, making light of it. 'Single, over thirty, living alone.' He held his hands up briefly, before starting on an onion.

Ellie nodded. After a moment's pause, she spoke again. 'So, your last girlfriend. Did you date her for a long time, then?'

Ray paused. 'Nearly three years,' he said.

'Oh, ages! Did you love her very much, then?'

Ray inwardly reeled slightly at this, but he took care to carry on chopping, steadily, rhythmically. He took a moment to reply. 'Yes, very much,' he said.

'What happened?' He did not reply. 'You can tell me,' she continued. 'If you want too.'

Ray stopped chopping and looked up at her. 'We broke up, that's all. Years ago now, really. She just moved on. I guess…I guess she just didn't feel the same way anymore. Nothing dramatic.' He looked up and smiled at her, but his eyes were cloudy. 'Fucking onions,' he said.

Ellie turned away from him and switched the channel. 'Humph,' she said. 'Her loss I reckon.'

***

Shortly after one of the goons had come in and removed her dinner tray, Rosie left the sitting room, moving swiftly through the bedroom and into the bathroom. She turned the taps and started filling the bath, ensuring that the water ran slowly. Stirring it a few times, she splashed the water around noisily, before removing her shoes and stepping up onto the bath rim. She stood there unsteadily for a moment, a hand held against the tiles, gaining her balance; then she unclipped the plastic cover above her. Gently hopping back down, she noisily swished the bath around again, ensuring that the water made as much noise as possible.

She took a deep breath. Once she started down this road, there was no going back and no possible way of undoing the damage. All afternoon she had been trying to rest and save her strength, but it had been futile; the knowledge of her escape plan had kept her in a state of tension, no matter how hard she tried to relax.

She picked up the roll-on deodorant she had been left and placed it in her right hand, upside down. It was a good fit and the bulbous end protruded from the bottom of her clenched fist, forming a make-shift hammer. Rosie had no idea how long it would last, but with the lid on it seemed a fairly tough, blunt instrument. In addition, she had the shampoo bottles as a backup, as well as her shoes. She was fairly lithe and would not need a huge amount of room to wriggle through.

She put the deodorant back down, closed the bathroom door and hopped back up and into position. She grasped hold of the plaster around the rim and started to pull, hard. Nothing happened, but a faint creaking sound from above her. Stopping for a moment, Rosie considered her options again. She did not want the whole ceiling to come crashing down!

Picking up the deodorant, she started bashing the plaster to one side of the hole. This was more successful and she started making dents in it, good dents, the plaster was definitely going to come away. She put the deodorant down, grasped the side of the opening and pulled with both hands again. Briefly, she swung, letting her whole weight strain the ceiling. She repeated the process, bashing, clawing, pulling, swinging and within a few minutes she had started making progress. Then a whole handful of plaster and lathe came down into the bath. Coughing, she stripped off her blouse and tied it round her face, before she set about her task again with a fixed, grim determination. She was going to get out of here.

Chapter 22

Ray had no sooner finished his dinner when his mobile rang. 'Caller Unknown' read the screen. He was tempted to let it ring out but he answered, wearily.

'This is Ray,' he said.

'Easy bruv.'

'Who's this?' Ray demanded.

'It's Ian. Ian Grant. You left me your card, remember? Few days back.'

'Yeah I remember. What can I do for you, Ian?'

'Other way round, bruv. And boy, have I got news for you!'

'Oh yeah?' Ray was less than enthusiastic.

'Might cost you though, know what I mean?' Ian chuckled. 'I'm sure you do.'

'What's this about, Ian? I'm tired and really not in the mood to fuck about.'

He heard Ian inhaling sharply. 'Bit tetchy, aren't ya? What's up, you boning the missus tonight or summin'?'

Ray did not reply. He was in no mood for a conversation with Ian Grant right now.

'Look here, right,' Ian continued. 'This is big. Proper. Gonna cost you a monkey, but it is *proper* big bruv, I'm tellin' ya.'

'£500? That's a bit out of your league, isn't it Ian?'

'There's people involved, right. *Non-national* people. You get me?'

Ray was interested now, despite himself. 'Like the sort of people we were talking about before?' he asked.

'Yeah, that's it. Look, if you want it, you gotta come and meet me, like *now* bruv.'

'Where?'

'Just park up down Grove Square, by the offy, yeah? We'll walk it from there. Fifteen minutes?'

'This better be worth it. I mean it,' said Ray, vehemently. 'Last thing I want to be doing right now is trawling the fucking red light district.'

'Don't bring the money now, I'll show you. Then you'll see.'

Slightly mollified, Ray agreed. 'I'll see you in fifteen,' he said and hung up.

He turned to Ellie. 'I have to go out. I made you up a bed in the spare room. Just go up when you want, all right?'

'Thank you,' she said and smiled. She looked tired. As he left the house, Ray smiled and found himself wondering why her simple 'thank you' had meant quite so much to him.

***

Rosie ran the water out of the bath, stripped off and had a brief shower. She actually needed it now, as she was covered in dust, dirt, plaster and mortar. Within five minutes she was washed, dried, and dressed.

She cleaned up the room as best she could, using one of the towels to sweep the floor and conceal all of the mess she had made. The hole above her was not very large, but it was big enough to get through. Then she opened the bathroom door, walking out and into the bedroom. With a clean towel wrapped around her, she went into the sitting room and turned on the television, loud enough so that anybody outside the sitting room door would be able to hear it. Casually, she returned to the bedroom and silently closed the partition doors. She returned back into the bathroom and shut that door. Should she lock it? She debated whether or not this was a good idea, before deciding against it. They might not notice the hole at first, after all, not many people would immediately stare up at the bathroom ceiling. At least try to keep them guessing for as long as possible, once they realized that she had escaped!

Rosie had knocked out the hole adjacent to the nearest joist she had been able to feel up above her in the dark. She planned to use this solid support to lever her way up and out of the bathroom.

It was not easy, but she was determined. First one elbow and her head went through, then the other elbow followed and her legs were pedalling air. Grunting, she inched and wriggled her way forward, over the beam. The effort pushed the air out her, before putting pressure on her stomach and then her uterus. She leant forward, panting, grunting, but getting up, slowly, inch by inch, until gravity had less of a pull on her and she was able to use her arms again, pushing down, straightening herself. With only her legs and backside left to follow, Rosie gathered her strength and quietly rolled over on her thigh, manoeuvring her posterior onto the joist, until, finally, she was sitting upon the attic beam, legs dangling down into the bathroom.

Grinning triumphantly, Rosie felt tremendously empowered. For a minute she sat there enjoying the moment, gathering her strength and waiting for her eyes to adjust to the darkness. Looking out over the vast expanse of attic that lay before her, Rosie began to realize that finding a way out was going to be tougher than she had anticipated. It was as black as pitch and only a matter of time before somebody raised the alarm.

***

Ian raised his head, almost imperceptibly, as Ray walked over to meet him. He fell in with Ray as he walked the street.

'Towards the docks,' he said, as they walked together.

'What's this about, Ian?'

'Shipping them in, init. Fuckers.'

'Sorry?' Ray stopped walking a moment and faced Ian on the pavement. 'Explain.'

'Nah, keep walking bruv.' Ian looked nervous. 'Serious, six o'clock, like.' Ian used his eyes to indicate the street behind them but his head did not move at all. Ray glanced swiftly behind them. Three large, black men were standing outside the off-licence, watching them walking away.

'Okay,' said Ray, resuming his walk. 'Why the hell did you want to meet here, anyway?'

'Dunno,' said Ian. 'Shithole, init.'

'Yes, it's the roughest part of the whole city. You must know that.'

'Hmm,' Ian replied. 'Don't come down here much. The thing is, right, I've been thinking.'

'Oh yes?'

'Yeah. I mean…what's it like, your job?'

This really did take Ray by surprise. 'You want to join the police force?' he said loudly, incredulous at the suggestion.

'NAH,' said Ian, laughing loudly. He pulled closer to Ray, 'Keep it down bruv, you trying to get me fucking mugged or summin'?'

'Sorry,' said Ray, reeling for the second time in as many hours. 'Erm…it's a good job, most of the lads are similar to you really, it's predominately male, white, working class…just normal people.'

'Is it? Cos you're quite posh, init.'

'Yeah, I am, compared to a lot of people that I work with, but certainly not compared to my top brass, no. But it's a massive organisation so you've got all sorts of people in truth. All sorts.'

'Hmm,' said Ian, scowling at the pavement. They walked on in silence for a minute or so before Ian spoke again. 'I don't want to be, like, pushing about bits and bobs forever, you get me?'

Ray threw his arms up. 'Of course, that's exactly what ninety percent of the people who joined the force worked out. Exactly that. But let me tell you, it's not easy. It's hard. In lots of ways, you know?'

'Like exams and shit?'

'Not so much that. Just, well, relationships can change.' Ray's thoughts flashed back over his past and the toll his job had taken on his personal life. He was not quite sure how to put it. 'So,' he continued, 'people you might have grown up with don't want to know you…that sort of thing. It's not something to go into lightly.'

'Nah, I been thinking about it. I don't want to just become a grass though, like be expected to turn everyone and that.'

'Well, that's partly what I mean. You have to make a choice, you can't walk both sides of the thin blue line, that's the worst of both worlds. Then you're never part of anything, neither one thing, nor the other. You either go straight, properly, or don't get involved with it. I'm not trying to put you off…'

'Nah, it's cool,' Ian interrupted him. 'You were pretty straight with me in the nick, I thought you would be straight up about it, that's all. So listen up. Tonight, well pretty soon actually, I heard there's a load of er…non-nationals, right, coming in the docks.'

'How could you possibly know that, Ian?' said Ray, his voice a mixture of suspicion and scepticism.

Ian stopped walking and faced him in the twilight. He paused, then shook his shaven head. 'Nah, I'm not into that mate. I don't want 'em here either. Take 'em out, yeah? Get 'em out of here.'

'You want them gone?'

'Fucking right I want them gone. Don't you?' Then Ian laughed loudly and pointed at him. 'You don't have to answer that but if you do, it will be used against you.' He laughed again and scrutinised Ray for a moment, squinting. 'They been shipping them in 'ere for months, right under your noses.' Ian tutted loudly and rolled his eyes. 'Come on PC Plod, I'll show ya.'

Chapter 23

Pitch black, blacker than an inkwell. Beyond the small radius of light afforded by the hole she had created, an expanse of invisible ceiling stretched out, hidden under a curtain of perpetual darkness.

Rosie swiftly realized that, without some form of lighting, finding a way down and out of this massive space was going to be nigh on impossible. Between the joists, heavy insulation had been set down over the lathe. Balancing on the thick, wooden beam, she began to lift the insulation. It was heavy work and the attic was sweltering. Slowly and steadily she walked along the joist, rolling up the heavy insulation. It made bare skin horrifically itchy and it was difficult to resist the temptation to drop it all and start fiercely scratching herself. Fortunately, she soon found what she was looking for and flung the insulation to one side, shuddering, she brushed off her arms.

Now uncovered, the spotlights infixed in the bathroom ceiling bled light up into the attic; illuminant stepping stones guiding her path. It was enough light to make the crucial difference. Looking around, she could see the vast space appeared completely empty. The far side of the attic was still shrouded in darkness, but it was of no consequence. There was a ladder no more than fifty feet from where she was standing, surrounded by a large, flat, space where boards had been laid down to create a temporary floor for storage in the past.

Swiftly, she scampered along the beams and made her way to the trapdoor. Perspiration ran into her eyes and the oppressive heat seemed to be intensifying. Rosie wiped her brow. The trapdoor was held in place by a small latch. She bent down over the trapdoor and pressed her ear to the wooden panels. Nothing was audible. She wondered briefly where the hatch might open, what may be below her; however, there was little time to consider that now. Time was of the essence! Sweating profusely, she stood on the floor behind it and, using her thumb, released the latch.

The heavy trapdoor swung down immediately, before she could grab it or stop it. Fortunately, although the drop was violent, it was virtually silent. The door did not swing or clatter into any adjacent walls below, simply dropped into position, the only noise a rush of air as it fell. Light flooded up and into the attic. Rosie was dripping now, sweat pouring freely off her nose, running down her forehead and stinging her eyes. She grabbed her blouse and wiped her face. The ladder was a two part affair, one section sliding up and on top of the other. Picking up the foot of the ladder, she dropped it quietly into position and it hung neatly, about a foot from the floor. Well-greased, it made no sound. Luck seemed to be on her side.

Descending, she found herself in an elegant corridor surrounded by plush red walls, wall mounted candelabras and various landscape paintings and portraits. Swiftly, Rosie grabbed the ladder from the base and started to shove it back up, jumping and pushing as she tried desperately to flip it back up and into position. It tottered, hanging in the balance, before gently sliding back down again. Already tired from her exertions, she tried once more, but it was no use. To push it back up and into the loft would require the use of some kind of pole. At 5'6" she was just not tall enough. And she was wasting time.

Rosie tried to fathom where she could be in this enormous house and tried to think clearly and calmly, but this was becoming increasingly difficult standing still in the corridor like a rabbit in the headlights. Her heart beat hard in her chest. Every second she delayed simply added to the likelihood that she would be seen. Hugging the wall, she ran on tiptoes down the corridor in front of her, her bare toes sinking into the luxury, red, deep pile carpet. The corridor ended in another, running at a right angles. Confused, she turned left. At the end of this passageway, she realized she had come the wrong way. In front of her the corridor ended, closed doors leading off on either side. She sprinted back the other way, retracing her steps back where she had come from, past the ladder and quickly onwards. The house remained quiet, her escape for now evidently still undiscovered. Half running, half walking, she kept moving on the balls of her feet.

To her right, the corridor suddenly gave way to a wide, sweeping stairway. She stood and peered down from her position on the top landing. Beautifully carved, dark wooden balustrades led down to the second floor in curving arcs. An identical stairway, smaller and within the arcs of the one above, ran down to the first floor. Rosie was aware that this was what was referred to, in architectural terms, as a Double Curved Grand Stairway. Below this, Rosie could see the stairs, balustrades and handrails leading up from the ground floor were marble, central and straight, covered in the same rich, deep carpet and built in the same style. A double entrance, left and right, led from the stairway onto the first floor landing. Directly opposite the foot of the marble stairs, across an enormous hallway, lay the grand entrance, an enormous oak, front door.

***

With no moon, the abandoned dockyard looked vast in the twilight. Ian led Ray quickly along the fencing before he stopped, abruptly. Directly above their heads, was a sign, still attached to the fence. PRIVATE - KEEP OUT. Ian pointed to it and sniggered, before whispering, 'Nice touch, init?' Then he pulled the wire fencing to reveal it had been cut away, neatly, by the post. He held it up to let Ray through, before following him into the restricted area.

Rusted machinery loomed large in the crepuscular light. Numerous warehouses were scattered about the complex, some dating back to the Victorian era, others had clearly been constructed more recently. Vast shapes and structures of broken, twisted metal conspired to lend an other-worldly feel to the place. A strange, foreign, extra-terrestrial landscape.

Keeping to the shadows, Ian led the way, half walking, half jogging. A big lad, he huffed and puffed a bit; however, much to Ray's surprise, Ian was evidently in reasonable shape. He kept it up for six or seven minutes, before he drew into the shadows of one of the many warehouses and approached the double doors. Squeezing through the gap in the doors with a grunt, Ian stopped inside and leant back on them. He used his weight to hold the doors apart for Ray, who followed him into the gloom.

This warehouse was one of the older structures, a red brick affair with tall, narrow windows that ran along each of the long walls.

Some of the windows had been bricked up, others were original and composed of many small panes, five across and seven upwards. Some of these individual panes were now smashed, but the majority were still there, decades of grime and filth entrenched into the glasswork.

Ian was dressed in black jeans, a grey T-shirt and a non-descript, hooded, black jacket. He lifted an elbow and put it through three window panes without flinching. The glass tinkled onto the concrete outside. Then Ian pulled out his phone and glanced at the screen. It read 20:25.

'Not long now,' he whispered.

Chapter 24

Rosie felt her heart pumping hard. Furtively, she started creeping down the staircase to the second floor. By the third step she was jogging, by the fifth she was running. The soft carpet cushioned her steps and she was soundless, undetected and close to freedom. Past the second floor, she hit the first floor landing at speed. At precisely that moment, there was a loud noise.

DING DONG.

The cheery sound echoed through the hallway below, bouncing off the walls and reverberating throughout the house. Rosie caught herself midstride and pulled back from the first floor landing, swerving into the corridor on her right. Desperately, she looked around, before she instinctively fled, running down the corridor as loud steps rattled smartly across the interior flagstones below.

The doors into each room were set back slightly from the passageways and Rosie squeezed herself into a doorway and stood on tip-toes, flat, back to the door. Screwing up her eyes briefly, she stood motionless, wondering whether or not to bite the bullet, open the door behind her and look for a proper hiding place. Her heart, hammered.

Somebody was greeted politely, briefly, the voices unclear. The front door closed and her ears followed two pairs of feet as they walked across the flagstones. The sound trailed away and she heard a door close. Muffled laughter followed.

Rosie took a few deep breaths. Knowing the back of the house faced roughly south, she now had managed to gather her bearings. The layout of the corridors on each floor appeared to be uniform. At that moment, she heard another door open, almost directly behind her.

The door was just around the corner of the corridor, presumably one of the rooms facing north, or north-east, and probably overlooking the driveway. The door closed with a slam and a man coughed, loudly. Within three strides he would round the corner and be face to face with her, hiding in the doorway.

Then there was a muffled curse and the door re-opened, noisily. Without a second thought, she sprinted down the corridor and kept on going, past the staircase, onwards and to the end of the passageway. She heard the door slamming again as she turned right at the end of the central corridor, heading up towards the north-west wing of the first floor. Panting, she put both hands to her face and stopped dead, trying desperately to control her breathing lest it gave her away. No sound was audible, thick carpet blanketing every step.

Seconds passed without incident. Then came a distant cough, from downstairs. Rosie returned, cautiously, peering round the corner, looking back into the central section of the corridor. The man was not there.

A door opened below and distant voices were briefly audible. The door below, closed. It was now or never.

Running, she took the final flight of stairs in less than ten seconds and began sprinting across the hallway, her bare feet slapping the cold stone floor, closing the gap. At that moment, a loud whirring, clicking sound began. Leaping in fright, Rosie instinctively ducked her head and kept on running, stretching out a hand to the heavy, oak front door, all that now stood between her and the outside world, separating her from freedom. Fearfully, she glanced behind her as a huge grandfather clock in the hallway began playing the Westminster chime, before it struck the hour.

DONG - DONG – DONG - DONG

Nobody there. As the clock struck nine, she clicked the latch.

***

Black clouds had been gathering overhead since the early afternoon and it was extremely muggy. Ray and Ian were standing, still sweating from their exertions, watching through the bust out panes of glass. As they waited, thunder rang out directly overhead, rumbling on for about fifteen seconds, before the heavens suddenly began violently hurling water onto the parched earth beneath it.

It was the first rain in weeks. The vantage point Ian had led them to overlooked the sea at a slight angle. A massive expanse of pitted concrete lay directly in front of them, whilst a gigantic slipway led into the sea to the right. It could have launched a cruise ship in its day and was truly enormous. Behind this space, a few more warehouses and storage units were visible, their shapes silhouetted against the dark sky. As chance would have it, the rain drove directly into their position and already the pair of them were getting rather wet.

'Nice job with the window,' said Ray, sarcastically. 'What the fuck are we doing here, seriously?'

'Watch,' Ian replied.

'I'm watching. How are they coming in, by parachute?'

Ian turned to him, a look of amusement on his face. 'Oh, funny fella, eh? Just keep your helmet on, you'll see.'

As they stood, a van appeared, lights off, driving slowly across the concrete towards the sea. As it did so, a small speedboat could be heard arriving, quietly chugging into the slipway. The van doors opened, six hooded men jumped off the boat and in less than thirty seconds the transfer was almost complete. Ray reached for his phone to call the station, but as he watched, loud shouts suddenly rang out across the concrete.

'Shit!' said Ian, quietly.

In an instant, more men poured onto the scene from the far side of their position, about half a dozen, waving bats, throwing bottles, one lit a petrol bomb and chucked it at the side of the van which promptly roared off with the back doors still open, spilling people out the back of it who scattered over the concrete in six different directions. Simultaneously, the speedboat rapidly reversed and sped away. Another man held up a brilliant torch and swept the area, neatly catching the pair of them in its full beam. With a shout, one of the aggressors pointed a baseball bat at the pair of them and Ian was already running before Ray had stuffed the phone back in his pocket.

'Go, go, go!' Ian shouted to Ray and suddenly Ray was running as fast as he was able, through the double doors and out into the night, panting and swearing at Ian who was a good twenty yards ahead of him and going like a man on fire. The rain was smashing down onto the concrete and the thunder let rip again, another deafening chord echoing across the city. As Ray took a fleeting glance back over his shoulder a flash of lightning lit up the scene and he saw one of the vigilantes gaining fast, swinging a chain around his head and running at full tilt towards the pair of them.

'Split,' screeched Ian and he veered off to the left, following the shadows and hugging the side of a warehouse. Ray kept on running, now genuinely frightened, before in a blinding flash he realized that he knew exactly where he was. To his right lay the recent crime scene, where the homeless junkie had died. This was definitely the same warehouse. Swerving right, Ray ran in through the warehouse doors and kept on going, past the stacks of empty crates and right to the back, into the shadows. As he stopped, he saw a figure standing at the front. Then another joined him and then, another. One held a chain, one held a bat and the other simply held his fist in his hand, menacingly. Together, the masked men strode into the warehouse and started to look for him.

Chapter 25

Having scouted the area before, it was now Ray who had the upper hand. Initially baffled as to how anybody could have got into the place, it had been Jason that had spotted the loose, corrugated iron panel. Ray remembered that it was on the back right, as he had looked in through the front doors. Making his way gingerly towards it, he heard a commotion outside, in front of the building. Now Ray could hear sirens faintly wailing in the background and he realized that either Ian, or somebody, had called the police and they were now on their way.

Emboldened, Ray ran quickly over to the loose panel and forced his way through, no longer caring about the noise he made. He kept on running, across the concrete and over to the iron, wire fence. Looking through it, he spotted Ian running from the scene. Hearing the thugs shouting behind him, Ray yelled to him in desperation and Ian turned around. Spotting who it was, he pointed to Ray's right and flashed a light towards him, yelling, 'The sign bruv, yeah? By the sign,' before hightailing it out of sight.

Ray remembered the sign. PRIVATE – KEEP OUT. He swiftly ran left and initially past it, before he spotted it, back-tracked and bowled out through the fence where the wire was cut away from the concrete pillar support. He heard a sharp ripping sound, the squad cars racing onto the scene in the background and, for the first time, Ray understood what it was like to be on the other side of the law. Adrenaline still pumping through his body, he jogged away through the pouring rain, crossing over Old Street and heading straight up the first road he came to, leading back towards Grove Square. Once safely up the side street, he slowed and started to walk, still catching his breath.

He soon realized that he was in the heart of the red light district. Girls appeared out of the darkness as he walked up the road. 'All right sweetheart?' said one, black stockings on scrawny legs, denim mini-skirt barely covering her arse. He glanced at her and cringed. Only crystal meth could do that to a human being. Clearly an addict, her face resembled a living corpse: tightly drawn, riddled with lines, eyes sunken, the emaciated skin covering her bones like a piece of withered parchment. 'You looking for a good time?' she said.

Ray shuddered and kept on walking. Another woman yelled at him across the street. 'Thirty quid for a suck or a fuck mate?' She laughed loudly, a cackle. Glancing over despite himself, he saw that it was just a girl, a teenager. Ray did not even know if she was joking or not. He suddenly thought of Ellie and panicked slightly. Who the hell had he let into his home? He put his head down and strode swiftly onwards, back to his car.

***

Opening the door, Rosie slipped out into the night, gently pulling the front door closed behind her. Ahead of her was a circular driveway that ran around some kind of ornamental statue, before leading down to some tall, black, metal gates. Convinced these would be electrically operated, Rosie ducked and ran left to the high, red brick wall that enclosed the entire property. Pulling into the shadows, she briefly considered her options.

Convinced that she was on an island, it initially seemed that the only way to get back to the mainland would be by boat. Although she kept fit swimming, and she certainly was a strong swimmer, Rosie conceded that the likelihood of making it from the Scilly Isles to the mainland were, at best, very slim. It was roughly the equivalent of swimming the English channel, from Dover to Calais. In the middle of the night and with potential rip tides out there, she reasoned the odds of making it were probably less than 100/1. Then it occurred to her; swimming across to a neighbouring island might actually be a realistic proposition. Once there, she would be able to raise the alarm somewhere and get back home.

The night was humid and dark, whilst the black clouds overhead signaled impending rain. Rosie scouted along the length of the wall as she jogged towards the end of the lawn, hoping there may be some supports, or a tree, that could be used to get out of the garden. She found nothing. Anxious to be on her way, she headed for the gates.

The iron gates looked like something from a tortuous nightmare, ludicrously tall with upwardly curving lines, gothic in style and with vicious looking spikes atop the pair of them. Aside them, stone pillars, apparently engraved with various animals, held them firmly in place. Rosie could dimly make out lions, chiseled into the white stone pillars, but some of the creatures engraved up the stonework were completely bizarre. However, there were no spikes atop the pillars and the strange, gothic carvings would serve well as footholds and handholds for a small and nimble person. She climbed swiftly and easily, her bare toes clinging onto the dry rock with ease. Clearing the pillar within a minute, she climbed carefully down the other side, jumping the final few feet.

Rosie was out.

Chapter 26

Within minutes of clearing the gates, Rosie had found her way down to the seashore. Her luck so far had been fantastic; however, it now seemed to be running out. The night was very dark and the storm clouds were gathering overhead in droves, blowing in on a stiff, easterly wind. The sea looked black, choppy and cold. A watery graveyard beckoning her in.

Looking out over the ocean, Rosie realized that she had no idea where she was at all. After clearing the gates, she had run right and now thought that she should be facing roughly east and, therefore, opposite the mainland. Standing on the beach in the dark, watching the inky, swirling waters breaking in front of her, she felt her heart sink. Not a light flickered in the blackness. Not even a fishing vessel, or a lighthouse, broke up the horizon.

The two Great Shearwaters that she had seen before did imply this was probably the Scilly Isles, certainly the western coastline. However, the whole of the western coast of the British Isles is littered with islands. From the Scilly Isles and travelling north, islands can be found in both the Bristol Channel and in St. George's Channel, with more dotted along the Welsh coastline and through into the Irish Sea. Yet more are situated outside Morecombe Bay in the form of the Piel Channel islands, whereas further out lies the Isle of Man. Shortly north of this landmark, the Scottish Isles begin, a further ninety-seven islands surrounding the rocky mainland. In addition, it was always possible that she was somewhere off the southern coastline. In truth, she had no idea.

Thinking hard, it occurred to Rosie that, surely, nobody would build such a house and a driveway, unless it was possible to drive somewhere. Many of these islands were connected to the mainland by roads that were only accessible at low tide. Perhaps this was one of them? In which case, her only realistic chance of escape was by following the road. Loath to follow such an obvious route, she saw no alternative. Reluctantly, she washed her bare feet in the cold sea water, before turning around and starting the precarious ascent back uphill to find the road that led from the house. As she climbed, it started to rain.

***

Ray opened his front door. Still fairly pumped, he went straight into the kitchen and poured himself a large whisky.

'Hi,' said Ellie. She was still on the sofa, watching the television. 'Blimey, where you been? Fight club?'

Ray looked down at his clothes. He was filthy and soaked, his dark jeans were smeared with some kind of vile, black goo and his shirt, once a mellow green, was torn and now ruined. Realizing his hands were also dirty, he put the drink down, walked over to the kitchen sink and washed them, thoroughly.

Ellie turned back to the television. Glancing at the digital clock on the oven, Ray realized that he had only been gone a few hours. It had felt like far longer. He exhaled heavily and picked up his drink, knocking half of it back, before swiftly going upstairs and changing. Returning to the living room, he found his drink again and collapsed on the sofa, next to Ellie. She looked a bit awkward and it then occurred to Ray; he had completely ignored her since walking in the front door.

'Sorry. Rough night,' Ray said.

'Are you okay? What happened to you?'

'I had a tip off, I went to investigate. Actually, you probably just saved me from getting my head kicked in.'

Ellie turned and faced him properly. 'Me?'

Ray downed his drink, before realizing he had not even offered her one. 'Sorry, do you want one?'

She pulled a disgusted face. 'Oh, no thanks. Whisky. Eugh!' That made Ray smile. Ellie continued, 'Well, don't leave me hanging. What happened?' Ray muted the television, then turned back to her.

'I was back in the old docks, I got a tip off that some people were being shipped in there, apparently it's been going on a while. Actually, you can help me out. Did you see people being moved around there?'

She looked genuinely confused. 'Erm…how do you mean?'

'People traffickers. People arriving in boats, people getting put into vans late at night? You ever see anything like that? Like, you know, illegals being shipped in on the sly, you get me?' Ray suddenly realized he had been hanging around Ian too long.

Ellie laughed at him. 'Yeah, I get you. *Bruv.*' She winked at him. 'But nah, I never saw anything like that, in fact I never saw anyone there at all. I dossed there for months, well about two months, before…well…before here.'

Both of them were quiet for a minute, wrapped up in their own thoughts. Ray broke the silence. 'Well, they were there tonight. Anyway, I got away.' Her eyes widened.

'Oh my God, did they chase you?'

'Yes. The police are not very popular in Tarnside, believe it or not.'

She looked away. 'No, I guess not.'

'I walked back up some dodgy road. I know areas of the city are rough, really, but…I don't know, I'm usually in a car. And I guess I'm not normally on my own. I wouldn't go down Grove Square on my own anyway.'

She looked across at him. 'Square is rough, not as bad as Roe Street though, that's pretty bad. I wouldn't go down there on my own either.'

'I think that's where I walked back up.'

'Probably, it's the quickest way from the docks to the Square.' She looked at him, knowingly. 'Rough, init.'

Ray stared at his empty glass. 'Yeah, really rough. Some of the working girls…' Ray shook his head. 'Just, well…just don't do drugs. Please,' he said.

Ellie looked slightly affronted. 'Why? What's it to you?'

'I'd say the same to anyone tonight, if it makes you feel better.' Ray stopped a moment in thought, before adding with a shudder, 'That face is going to haunt me.'

'Oh…you saw the meth heads!' Ellie chuckled. Then she added, 'Bit soft for a copper, aren't you?'

Ray looked back at her. 'Caring about other people isn't a weakness, you know,' he said. 'One of the hookers looked younger than you.' Ellie shifted, awkwardly, in her seat. She stared back at the mute television.

'I don't want you to end up like the woman I saw tonight, that's all.'

'Well,' Ellie said, 'that's sweet. I'm gonna hit the sack.' She got up. 'Night night.'

'Yeah, we're up at five.'

'Huh?' She looked suitably horrified.

'You owe me, remember? I need you to identify the guy you scored off.'

'Oh…right. It was a guy called Tony, down on the Square. That's all I know, anyway, to be honest. Sorry.' She smiled, sweetly.

'Great, that should narrow it down when you look through the photos down the nick. And I'm on early turns this week.' Ray grinned at her. 'So, sleep tight.'

Chapter 27

The wind had picked up and the rain was coming down in bucketfuls. Rosie trudged through the downpour, her feet cold on the wet tarmac. She had started out jogging, but that had been twenty minutes ago. Now she was starting to feel extremely tired; her exertions so far tonight had taken a lot out of her. The road was surrounded by trees and scrubby bushes, obscuring the views, whilst visibility on the route ahead was reduced to a vaporous murk.

Even the birds seemed uneasy. A seagull suddenly started screaming somewhere to her left, before flying directly over her head in a flap of feathers, its high pitched cries eerily piercing the night. Rosie wondered what had spooked it quite so badly. Once again, she increased her pace. No foxes here. No dogs either. *Just a stupid bird.* At that moment, lightning flashed across the sky, followed by a distant peal of thunder. The rain carried on, relentless. Black clouds raced past a luminous moon.

Ten minutes later, the road forked. No signs, no clues. The road simply divided, one fork left, one fork right. The road so far had not been perfectly straight and Rosie was tired and lost and confused. She did not even know if the house was directly behind her anymore, whether she was facing north or west or east. Hoping for the best, she opted for the right fork, trusting it would lead roughly east and back towards the mainland. Within five minutes, the road had ended in a slipway. She was back at the seashore, staring at a savage sea.

The storm was certainly picking it up. The waves had grown angry, white topped surf spewed against the rocks beneath her feet. Further to her right lay a rocky outcrop and the waves were smashing up against it, sending plumes of spray high into the sky. Another peal of thunder rang out, the noise echoing off the sea beneath it. It rolled on and on for about twenty seconds, reverberating around the rocky cliffs and ending in a boom, with a huge flash of lightning. The wind was starting to whistle over the rocks, audible, a living, breathing beast. A gust spun itself about her, caught her, wrapping itself all around her slender frame, buffeting her, shaking her, before she was released as it passed on its way. The electric storm was becoming a gale.

Unsure of what to do next, Rosie stood in the centre of the road at the top of the slipway, staring out across the sea, hands on her hips while the wind blew all about her. She felt terribly isolated. This was not how she had imagined things working out. Why the first storm in months had felt the need to break tonight, she had no idea, but she cursed her luck. It was the worst possible eventuality that she could have envisaged. It was little wonder she had seen nothing out at sea, with this forecast to blow in!

The rain was not warm, just sheets of cold water pouring down, mercilessly. She shivered violently, realizing that if she did not keep moving she may become seriously cold, or worse. She wrung out her hair with shaking hands, before turning to retrace her steps. Then she saw the headlights.

Rosie broke left, sprinting to take refuge in the rocky cliffs as powerful beams swept across the slipway. Thoughts flashed through her mind. How had they had found her? Had they followed her? There must be a reason they had come down here. Was she in the right place after all, was this the way out at low tide? Was there a boat moored here?

She heard shouts behind her as she scrambled over the rocks, desperately trying to escape. There was nowhere to hide here, nowhere to go to, except across the rocks that bordered the coastline. Powerful torch beams danced around her and she knew that she had definitely been spotted. Why had she stood there, in the middle of the bloody road?

Briefly, she looked at the angry swell and considered leaping into it, swimming away from her tormentors. She could probably swim better than any of them. Further too. Reaching a rocky ledge, she stopped. She stood. She looked back at the two men on her tail, the closest was just twenty feet or so away. She raised her hands to dive.

'Don't do it, you'll fucking die! Don't be stupid woman, nobody even wants to hurt you for fuck's sake!' he yelled. The man had stopped chasing her. He stood, panting. 'Rosie, there's no way out that way. Unless you plan to swim to France?'

She stood, poised, uncertain. Then she lowered her arms. There was no way out that way. The game was up.

'Well fuck you,' she shouted back. Prepared to give herself up, she turned around and faced him. Then something intangible overtook her rationale and in a moment of blind insanity she turned back to the sea and jumped, high and far, crashing down into its flailing arms.

A million freezing needles pierced her skin as she plunged into the black depths, swallowed up instantly by the foaming waters. Deep, deep down, suddenly she felt her feet touch bottom and instinctively she pushed back, fighting, kicking, up, up, through the water, bubbles streaming from her nose.

Finally breaking the surface, she saw the man was standing directly in front of her. 'You fucking lunatic!' he exclaimed. He knelt down and offered his hand. 'Come on, get out. Before you bloody freeze to death!'

Chapter 28

Ray had not been joking and was bashing on Ellie's door at four-thirty in the morning.

'Rise and shine sleepy head,' he shouted. 'Or I'll drag you out butt naked!' Unsure as to whether Ray was joking or not, Ellie gave a muffled shout in reply, stating she had nothing to wear. 'Not a problem,' Ray called back, 'you'll fit right in. And if you help me identify this Tony fella, I might even buy you some clothes later.'

Ellie opened the bedroom door and stuck her head out, eyes still half closed. Ray was crossing the landing into the bathroom, wearing only his boxer shorts. 'If it's anything like your taste in shirts, I'll choose my own thanks,' she said, before shutting the door again.

'Fifteen minutes,' he said, before realizing that she had just seen him virtually naked. Oh well, never mind, he thought. Ray was no prude.

'I can't eat this early, but we'll get a fry up later on, if you like. Well, I plan to have one,' he called, briefly washing his face. He crossed back over the tiny landing into his bedroom, calling out, 'Bathroom is all yours.'

'Okay, great,' she called back. 'That's just great. Thanks so much.'

Fifteen minutes later and they were both in the car, driving to the station. 'I can't believe you have got me up, it's like the middle of the night,' she grumbled.

'Ah, you get used to it,' Ray replied, cheerfully.

'I don't want to get used to it, thank you. I'm really not a morning person.'

'Well lucky for you that this is just a one-off then,' he replied. 'I have to do this all the time.' He swung the car round a corner. 'Nearly there now.'

'Humph,' she said, crossing her arms. Then she put a hand to her head. 'I can't believe we are awake. Seriously. Can't you let a girl get a little sleep?'

Ray sniggered slightly. 'Well…that all depends.'

'Oh, please!' Ellie turned to the window to hide her smile.

They pulled into the station and parked the car. Ray took her in through the back entrance and into one of the interview rooms, which held a table and three chairs. He fetched her a coffee and then disappeared again, shortly returning with a computer tablet. 'Right,' he said. 'Here are all the Tonys on the system that are known dealers on our ground. Flick through, take your time. I've got better things to do than sit here watching you, but when you find him just go tell the Duty Sergeant and he'll get hold of me, all right?'

'Who?' she said, still grumpy. Ray opened the door and pointed down the corridor.

'That geezer,' he said, pointing.

'Right,' she said, sighing.

'See you in a bit,' Ray said, closing the door. He left instructions with the Duty Sergeant not to let her out the station, just in case Ellie decided that she wanted to leave without co-operating. Ray then proceeded to his desk to tidy up some loose ends. The body in the warehouse had been identified as Michael Caplin and Ray had paperwork to complete for that case. It seemed a fairly straightforward heroin overdose and Ray prepared his notes accordingly, although he would need the autopsy report before he could officially close the file.

Ray then looked over the video evidence that Jason had marked for his attention. A heavy-set, oafish looking man wearing a black leather jacket had been caught on the CCTV, walking towards the scene at about the right time. It was possible that Jason had correctly identified one of the men who had attacked John Harrington in the Fish 'n' Chip shop, but Ray did not recognize him. Jason had made extensive enquiries the previous day and had also failed to get a name. Jason's notes evidenced that he had even tried the digital, facial recognition database, which many officers privately considered hopeless, but it had all been to no avail. The lead was tenuous anyway, but without an ID on the suspect it was of no use at all at the moment. The other two Detective Constables had failed to find any eye witnesses who would admit to having seen anything, which did not surprise Ray a great deal. In addition, John Harrington had no form. Why anybody had entered his shop and stuck his arms in a fat fryer, remained a mystery for the moment.

Ray returned to see how Ellie was getting on. She was still looking through the database as he opened the door. She looked up as he entered and nodded, before scrunching up her forehead again and returning to her task.

'There's a lot of faces here, Ray,' she said. 'It's getting a bit confusing.'

'Do you know any of them?' he asked. She looked a bit overwhelmed.

'I think so. Well, I don't know them really, just seen them around, you know.' She looked up at him and her forehead cleared again. She pushed the tablet away from herself.

'Yes, well, they are mostly local so that's not surprising,' Ray said. 'Tarnside is a big place, a lot of people live here.'

'Yeah.' There was a short pause. 'I think I found him though,' she blurted out, unexpectedly.

'Oh right! Great!'

'Yeah, it's number fifty-eight.'

***

Detective Chief Superintendent Manson was in his office, staring out of the window. 'So, they found the van then?' he enquired of the Detective Superintendent in his office.

'That's right guv,' Paul replied. 'Burnt to a cinder last night, down the old dockyards.'

'I see. Useless then.' His tone was icy.

'Yes guv. Well, at least we know that they are still in the area. Or at least one of them.'

It was rare for Albert to let his emotions boil over at all, especially in front of another officer, but his voice was rising. 'Where did the van come from? It can't have just appeared there.' He turned to face his deputy, who immediately saw that he was absolutely livid. Albert promptly exploded, 'So where the fuck did it come from, Paul?'.

'We don't know guv. It was probably driven there with different plates, in which case the automatic plate recognition software would not have picked it up.'

'I am fully aware of the limitations of the ANPR system.' Albert's eyes flashed with anger. 'I understood that uniform was under strict instructions to stop and search anything that even remotely resembled the van in question. Besides, why do you suppose these people left the number plates for us to find?'

Paul was beginning to resent his cross-examination. 'I really don't know, guv. Do you?' he said, flatly.

'No,' he snapped. 'I don't. It looks like they just want to piss me off. Making us look like a bunch of wankers up here. This whole station is turning into a…it's a bloody circus out there,' he ended furiously, pointing towards the Incident Room dealing with Rosie's abduction. Paul looked at the floor. He privately agreed with his superior, but did not feel he could really say so just at the moment. Albert walked over stiffly to Paul and spoke quietly. 'We're running out of time, Paul. Thirty-six hours. You do know what they threatened to do if we don't comply?'

Paul nodded. 'I know. They threatened to kill her, guv.' Albert was still steaming, but he dropped his voice and hissed his reply.

'If only, Harding. They are going to torture her, live over the internet, until we pay up. Some vile idea they got off some horror movie. I don't know why people make this shit, it just gives people sick ideas. And now we have some mindless bastard who actually wants to make it a reality.'

Paul was taken aback. 'That's not what I understood from the note the Super gave me,' he replied.

Albert swung about, walked behind his desk and retrieved a sheet of paper, in a plastic, transparent, A4 envelope. He waved it, before slamming it on his desk with his hand. 'This is the real document, Paul. The one we gave the team, that was in case the story got leaked. We might have a publicity ban in the UK when it comes to ongoing kidnappings, but that doesn't stop the internet news reels from publishing whatever they can get their hands on.' He paused, breathing heavily. 'You begin to see where this is heading? And why they've asked for so much fucking money?'

'They want us to call their bluff,' said Paul, glumly.

'Precisely. And think of the precedent that would set. Not to mention the public outrage.' Albert bent over his desk. 'And who do you think the public are going to blame?' He let the words hang in the air for a moment, letting Paul absorb the news and the potential repercussions. Then he continued.

'Can you even *imagine* the public reaction if these bastards start broadcasting it, live, to all and sundry, whilst we sit here, refusing to pay?' Albert paused again, standing upright, furious. His eyes glittered as he clenched his fists by his side. 'You see?' He pointed a stiff arm to the window, pointing to the streets below. 'It'll be fucking carnage out there.'

Chapter 29

'Tony Parkes?' Frank was standing in his office, looking at the photo in his hand. He looked haggard and Ray wondered when he had last been home.

'That's right, guv,' Ray replied. 'I have a witness. She's ID'd him as the guy who supplied her with the China White. And he's got form for dealing.'

'Not for a long time now, though.' Frank sat down at his desk, still staring at the photograph. He looked up. 'Are you sure this is the right man, Jackson?'

In truth, Ray was not convinced that it was the right man. Nagging doubts remained in his mind about Ellie and her reliability as witness. He had not even broached the matter of her testifying in court if they failed to find any drugs on Tony Parkes, or at his home. Ray also knew a decent lawyer would rip Ellie's credibility to pieces if they got a whiff of her background history, let alone the fact she had recently been hospitalized on the toxicology ward. He also remained unclear as to why, if she had already identified the right man, she was still looking through the potential suspects when he had entered the interview room.

'I think we should pull him in and give his place a spin, guv.'

Frank seemed reluctant. There was a brief, tense silence before he relented. 'Fine,' he said, 'bring him in. You can spin him under PACE. Take Jason with you and ask the skip for a couple of uniform. They'll enjoy that.' PACE referred to the Police and Criminal Evidence Act 1984. There have been various modifications to the Act, but various clauses allow for the legal search of premises when a suspect is arrested for specific offences, without the need for a separate search warrant from the magistrate's court.

'Yes guv. Thanks.' Ray ducked out of the office and swiftly made his way downstairs, intending to find the Duty Sergeant and sort out a few uniform. On the way, he remembered Ellie was still downstairs and that neither of them had had any breakfast yet. Ray told Jason to be ready to go out in an hour, then sought out the Duty Sergeant and arranged for his back-up to be ready. Finally, he collected Ellie from the interview room. Feeling a bit flash, he had grabbed the Audi keys, but she didn't seem to notice; simply got in the car without a second glance. Ray briefly wondered why he was trying to impress a girl ten years his junior. Stupid, really.

'Right,' he said, as they buckled up. 'Time for breakfast.' Her forehead told him that something was on her mind. 'Spit it out then,' he said, starting the engine.

She looked over at him disdainfully, before returning her gaze to the view ahead and sticking her nose in the air. 'As it happens,' she began slowly, 'I did have something on my mind.'

'Uh huh,' said Ray. 'I figured.' As he waited for the electric gates to open, Ellie gave him another long look. Despite trying to look haughty, her blue eyes were smiling. Then clouds crossed her face and she looked quite concerned again. 'What's the matter?' said Ray, pulling out onto the road.

'I was thinking, you're gonna want me to go to court maybe. I don't want to do that,' she said, flatly. This was clearly not up for negotiation.

'No, that's okay,' he replied. 'I thought about that as well, earlier on. If we don't find any drugs and he denies it, then there is no way the CPS will let us take it to court anyway. And if we do, then we won't need your testimony anymore. We'll have the evidence to show the court.' Ray glanced over at her in the passenger seat and noticed she looked unconvinced. Then he narrowly missed a cyclist and concentrated on driving again. 'All right?' he asked.

'You sure?'

'Yep.'

'So, what now, then?' Ellie paused. 'I guess you're gonna drop me off somewhere, huh?'

Now Ray understood what was really on her mind. He made light of it. 'Oh, no fucking chance,' he replied. 'It's your turn to do dinner tonight.'

Ellie looked over to him and smiled. 'I'm a shit cook,' she said.

***

Rosie was back in the mansion, back in the same quarters where she had begun. The bathroom still had a hole in the ceiling, but the men had put some boards over it and heavy weights on top of those. They had also informed her that the trapdoor out of the loft was now bolted and padlocked. Strangely, they had not seemed angry with her; in fact, since her recapture, the men had all treated her with a great deal of respect. Clearly, they had been genuinely impressed by her ingenuity. However, they were now very much on their guard. Rosie doubted that whoever was running this outfit had taken quite so kindly to her little escapade.

The man who had helped her get out of the sea the previous evening had been very kind. He had immediately covered her wet, white blouse, now quite transparent, with his own jacket, picked her up like a baby and carried her back to his car. Freezing cold and shivering violently, Rosie had simply clung onto him, wondering if she was hypothermic yet. Within ten minutes she had been back in her room and standing under a hot shower.

She had now given up escaping, at least for the time being. Last night had been a fairly horrific experience, she had been frozen, half-drowned and ultimately got absolutely nowhere. She had also got the impression last night that, for whatever reason, the men did not mean her any harm. As frustrating and puzzling as this was, Rosie resigned herself to the fact she would be freed when these thugs had sorted out whatever it was they were doing. Why it involved her, however, she still had no idea. She presumed that they had originally abducted the wrong person. She then wondered who had been assigned to work on Operation Virtus, back at the station. If she had not been the right target, then maybe these goons were still after somebody else…

Chapter 30

'Police, open the door!' Ray bashed on the front door with his fist. 'Open this door, NOW!' Uniform were already round the back of the terraced property, while Jason and Ray were standing at the front. Nobody appeared to be home.

Ray stood back from the door, then walked the few steps back to the front gate. It was a battered, knee high, wooden affair, clinging on by a single hinge. Listing, half open, Ray gave it a kick and it broke away completely, the rusty, metal peg on the concrete pillar finally snapping at the base.

Ray turned to the house and cupped his hands. 'OPEN THIS DOOR PARKES,' he bellowed. Suddenly, Jason shifted into action, clocking through the gears like a well-oiled machine as he sprinted off down the pavement. Ray turned as the young Detective Constable hurtled past him, just in time to see Tony Parkes drop a burger and start running.

'Son of a BITCH!' Ray exclaimed. He snatched the radio from his pocket. 'This is India Juliett one five two calling Delta Whisky, suspect is fleeing the Parkes' house, heading up Dibden Street towards Brook Hill, India Tango three nine nine in pursuit on foot, advise all units we have a warrant on the suspect, a Tony Parkes. In pursuit.'

Ray heard the siren of the squad car behind the house wailing into action as he wrenched open the car door and stuck the keys into the ignition. Chucking the radio onto the passenger seat, he heard Dispatch confirming his report. Instantly, Ray knew every spare unit in Tarnside would be switching on the blues and roaring towards the scene. Uniform did enjoy a good chase and Ray missed it dearly. CID was good, he had no regrets about making the transfer, but his first few years tearing about in the squad car were still some of his fondest memories. But then, he reflected, it had been a happier time for him in many ways.

'Coming. Ready or not!' said Ray through gritted teeth, grinding the vehicle into first gear. Flicking on the lights and the siren, he blazed out into the street with a screech of smoking rubber, flooring the pedal as he tore down the road, determined to nail the bastard who thought selling lethal grades of heroin to teenagers was somehow okay. Ray knew that Ellie had only had a small amount of it; otherwise there would have been two corpses in the warehouse that day.

The northern end of Dibden Street ended in a standard T junction where it met Kings Road. Braking violently at the end of the street, Ray saw Jason ahead of him, tumbling over a back fence of the house directly facing the end of Dibden Street. The gate leading round the house and into the back garden was still rocking on its hinges. Ray smacked the steering wheel in frustration, punched on the satellite navigation system and took a left turn, gambling that he could find a way round the houses and onto a parallel highway behind Kings Road.

In the rear view mirror, Ray caught sight of the squad car racing up the road behind him. Cursing, he grabbed the radio and reported what he had just seen. Within ten seconds the squad car behind him was doing a rapid three point turn, before it screamed off in the opposite direction, fully lit up, sirens on the rapid call, known as the 'Yelp'. Ray flicked a switch, changing from the stretched, rising and falling tone, the 'Howl', to mirror the 'Yelp' call of the squad vehicle, police protocol when negotiating blind corners and junctions at speed. The satellite navigation system had not yet obtained a fix and remained greyed out, searching, while Kings Road seemed to stretch endlessly into the horizon. Not a road that Ray was familiar with, it was turning out to be an extremely long and straight route. As he motored down the street, Jason's voice crackled over the radio, sounding like he was having some kind of asthma attack.

'India Tango…three nine nine,' came the wheezing voice. 'I've lost him, guv.'

*

Upon arriving back at the station, Ray was immediately accosted by the Duty Sergeant. 'Detective Superintendent wants to see you,' he was told. 'In his office. Wouldn't keep Harding waiting if I were you.'

Making his way upstairs, Ray knocked and a voice called him in. He sidled into the room where Paul was stood, facing the window and looking across the grey city beneath. The rain continued to patter down intermittently and it was cool outside, defying the weather predictions of an Indian summer. Ray closed the door.

'John Harrington. I last nicked him for dealing oh, six, seven years ago now. Dirty little toe rag.' Paul sniffed and glanced briefly over at Ray. 'Spent about a month doing obbos on him, early turns, late turns, nights. Six weeks I spent gathering evidence, one way or another. His brief got him off, little bastard. Oh well,' Paul continued, grinning, 'out of the fire and into the frying pan, by the looks of it.'

'What was he pushing?' asked Ray.

'Oh, all sorts. Everything from skunk to the Big H. Regular little pick 'n' mix he had going on.' Paul turned and faced him. 'I'm sorry I haven't been able to assist you very much. Obviously the other case has to take priority.'

Ray simply nodded. Paul continued, 'I heard you got a lead on the China White. Well done.'

'He got away, guv. We couldn't catch him.' Ray looked at the floor, feeling his face flushing slightly.

'Don't worry. That happens. Tony Parkes will turn up.' He looked up at Ray and held his eye. 'I want you to leave that alone for now. Concentrate on Harrington and finding his killer. Parkes can wait. Clear?'

'Yes, guv.'

Paul paused a moment, before sitting down behind his desk. He motioned to the chair in front of him and Ray sat down.

'Good,' Paul said. 'So, fill me in. Have you heard back from the pathologist yet? Did forensics turn up anything else at the scene, other than these footprints? And what about this CCTV lead?'

'I should hear from the pathologist today, but no official word as yet. The CCTV lead is unsubstantiated and the suspect, if you can call him that, is not known to us. Forensics didn't turn anything else up, and we have no witnesses. We didn't find anything incriminating at the scene, but then, I didn't think we would, to be honest.'

'No?' Paul queried. He had his own theories on the matter, but he wanted to see what the Detective Sergeant was thinking.

'Well no, guv. I mean, if someone was sticking your hands in a fat fryer, I think you'd probably tell them what they wanted to know.'

'So if he was hiding something…' Paul prompted him.

'It's long gone,' Ray concluded.

Paul nodded his assent. 'Yeah, I would run with that. Was the till cleaned out?'

'Yes guv.'

'But this is a bit more than a robbery gone wrong, wouldn't you say?'

It was then that Ray realized he was being tested, at least to some extent. He chose his next words carefully.

'Well, we know there were at least three people there, presumably men as they held him and forced his hands into the fryer, which can't have been easy. From the footmarks, we can see they stood around him, I'm guessing one on each arm and one clearly stood behind him. The back door is like Fort Knox so, unless it was wide open which seems pretty unlikely given the effort that's been made to secure it, three men came in the front door. It seems more likely to me that they would have entered at, or near, closing time. Otherwise people coming to buy their fish 'n' chips might have come along and seen something at the time.' Ray paused.

'Right,' Paul agreed. 'Look, here's what I think. John Harrington was a low life, a real shit bag. He sold to anyone and everyone, used to tap up girls on A-bombs down the old docks back in the day…'

'A-bombs?' queried Ray, interrupting.

Paul looked at him as though he had just grown a second head. 'Yeah, A-bombs…I thought you worked on that den down Brook Hill for months?'

'I did. But I never heard of an A-Bomb. Sorry.'

'It's when you wrap heroin and marijuana in a paper together. So the kids would think it was just a spliff, right?'

'Oh right, yes. I know what you mean now. That's a sick trick to play on anybody.'

'Sick, right? A long time back now, I suppose, they used to hold raves down the docks, in the disused warehouses. They were popular, people came down from all over. There were far too many people for us to do anything much, except wait 'til it had finished. And the laws were different back then.' Paul paused a moment, his memory flashing back to the enormous parties and the illegal rave scene, where he had worked undercover for almost a year. He shook the memories from his mind and refocused on the Detective Sergeant standing in front of him.

'Anyway, this scrote was often seen down there, selling gear.' Paul paused again. 'Look, basically, he was always mixing with the younger teens, getting the young girls high, right? But nothing was ever proven.'

'I see,' said Ray.

'Looking at the M.O here and knowing Harrington's form, I think this is probably an act of retribution; he was either into someone for a lot of money or he had dealt drugs to somebody's kid or something like that. Whoever did this may have been hired or it might have been personal. Maybe start asking around down the Fir Garden, if you can get near the place.'

'You think this could be a Traveller incident?'

'It's possible. They like to sort things out themselves, you know, send a message. And whoever did this is definitely sending a message out to the street.'

Chapter 31

Jason caught up with Ray as he sat down at his desk with a sandwich. He was stood with Mitchell Wright, one of the Detective Constables assigned to Ray's taskforce for the murder enquiry. 'Guv, have you heard the latest?' Jason said.

Ray looked up sharply. 'Is there news on Rosie Blake?'

'Oh, no. Nothing on that score. Sorry,' Jason replied, a little awkwardly. He barely knew the missing Detective Inspector and now he felt bad for having put his foot in it with such a clumsy remark.

'Oh. Well, what's new then?'

'Another body has just been reported, about five minutes ago. Near Grove Square, on Roe Street. Do you know it?'

The haggard face Ray had seen the previous evening came flooding back into his mind's eye. He stared at his pallid chicken and mayonnaise sandwich, laid out on white bread.

'Otherwise known as hoe street,' said Mitchell, which made Jason laugh. Ray did not feel like joining in the banter. Not for the first time, Ray wondered if he really fitted in with the police force. He wondered if he really fitted in anywhere.

'Guv?' It was Jason again. 'You hear me?'

'Yes, I heard you. I'm just going to finish my lunch and then…' Ray put his sandwich down, no longer hungry. He picked up his coat. 'I take it this is another heroin overdose?'

'Yep,' said Mitchell. He then turned to Jason and started singing, making gun shapes with his hands, '*Boom – boom - boom. Another hoe bites the dust.*'

'Yes, thank you DC Wright,' said Ray, testily. 'You and Rachel can start on those footprints, I want to know the make and size of every print recovered by forensics at the scene and by the end of the day. Jason, you're with me.'

Ray started walking towards the door, glancing over his shoulder in time to see Jason waving and smiling sarcastically at Mitchell, who was giving him the finger. Suddenly spying Ray had turned his head, Mitchell stopped immediately and started turning pink.

'Oh, not you, guv,' he said. Ray halted, propping the door ajar for Jason who kept walking, sphinx-like, out of the room. Ray stood there for a moment, watching Mitchell turning red. He pointed at him and stared down his finger. 'End of the day, Mitchell,' he said, before turning and leaving the office, the double doors swinging in his wake. Walking down the corridor, Ray managed to smother his laughter.

*

Ray exited the vehicle and put his hood up against the rain that was pattering down onto the pavement. Blocks of three-storey flats lined the street, dirty, net curtains shielding the occupants behind their oversized panes of glass. Litter had collected in the gutters: crisp packets, cans, cigarette packets, polystyrene containers that had once held fast food. The concrete breeze blocks had been given a uniform, shingle cladding, in an attempt by the original designers to give the road a coastal air. Unfortunately, the effect was universally drab, serving only to accentuate the monotony of the featureless, grey buildings and further contribute to the depressing environment.

The scene was already cordoned off by the time Ray and Jason arrived and there was a large uniform presence, although Roe Street now appeared completely deserted. Exterior stairwells ran up to the flats, all iron handrails and white painted concrete. At the foot of one of these stairwells a woman lay, face down in a pile of vomit, eyes permanently closed. The pair of them walked briskly to the scene.

Vomit mingled with the reek of urine and faeces producing a toxic stench. Ray covered his nose as he stared down at the body. Her wet hair was plastered down onto her head, black, stringy hair and not enough of it to cover the white scalp underneath that now resembled pallid rubber. She was wearing a soiled, blue, denim jacket and a shiny, black skirt, which was so short the bottom of her arse and vaginal crack were visible. Both looked red and sore, small, red welts scattered across the skin. Scrawny and thin, her white legs lay at abnormal angles on the ground, like broken sticks. Her left arm lay outstretched on the concrete, palm upwards, the skin covered in track marks from previous injections.

'Fucking hell,' said Jason. 'I pity the poor fucker that has to clean that up.' His face was a picture of absolute disgust. 'Fucking stinks. I don't know what's worse, the puke, the piss, or the dog shit she's stuck her hand in.' He turned away and walked back a few steps. His reaction made Ray laugh.

'Get your gloves on, DC Stephenson,' he said, with deliberate, feigned enthusiasm. 'It's time for a closer examination!'

'You can f…' Jason caught himself.

'And less of the potty mouth, thank you. Occasional swearing is one thing, but you're turning it into a regular hobby. Sooner or later, you might just open your mouth and say the wrong thing to the wrong person. Know what I mean?'

'Yes, guv. Right. Anyway, she can't have cooked that shit up here. I mean, prepared the, you know…' he tailed off.

Ray gave him a look, walked back to the car, fetched a box of latex gloves and returned to the scene. He handed a couple of pairs to Jason and donned two pairs himself. 'I always wear two,' Ray told him. 'Just in case.' He bent down and was about to check the woman's pockets, but something made him draw back. Ray walked over to the uniformed Constable and asked him if the police photographer had been down yet, or the divisional surgeon. Apparently, neither had yet been on scene. Happy to have a reasonable excuse to leave the body alone, Ray returned to Jason, who was standing back at the edge of the cordon, and imparted the news.

'What now then?' Jason asked. 'Shall we wait?'

Ray ignored the question. 'Who reported the body, anyway?'

'Anonymous,' Jason replied.

'Well, you're right about one thing, she didn't sit down here cooking up a shot under the stairwell. Well, it's possible I suppose, but it seems pretty unlikely.'

'You think she was dumped here?'

'I don't know. She's vomited, so she must have been alive here. It seems pretty unlikely someone would just dump her and leave her there, in that state. Even if there is a shooting gallery round here, which wouldn't surprise me in the least, if she was still alive then normally someone would call an ambulance; even if they didn't hang about to watch it arrive.'

'Yeah, I see what you mean,' said Jason, thoughtfully. 'Unless she was trying to get help herself. Maybe she knew something was wrong, that she had OD'd?'

'Yes,' Ray agreed. 'That's more likely. Most overdose victims don't fall into an immediate coma, anyway. It's often a prolonged process: breathing becomes slower, the brain becomes damaged through lack of oxygen until, eventually, the person dies. Which means she was probably using in this block of flats.' Ray looked up at the building. 'And that she was on her own when she shot up. Realised she had overdosed. Staggered out the flat, down the stairs, collapsed, vomited, died.' Ray looked at Jason. 'Let's take a walk,' he said.

The pair of them walked back to the stairwell where the dead woman lay. Ray passed her and walked up the stairs. The whole stairwell had been cordoned off. Three storeys stood above the ground floor with ten flats on each, leaving a total of thirty flats to eliminate. Starting with the first floor, Ray and Jason started knocking.

Within an hour and a half, they had eliminated twenty-five of the flats from their enquiries. Now on the third floor and about to knock on the final door, Ray's mobile phone rang. Retrieving it from his pocket, he looked down and saw it was the station. Strange they were not using the radio. He answered it. 'Raymond Jackson.'

'Ray, it's Frank. Are you at the scene on Roe Street?'

'Yes. The divisional surgeon has been now, so has the photographer. It's a straightforward OD by the look of it.'

'I don't doubt it.' Frank sounded tense. 'The thing is, there's been another report.'

'Another body?' Ray enquired. He heard Frank exhaling loudly.

'Yes,' Frank replied. 'And the Press are going to be all over this one. It's Courtney Tumbler.'

Chapter 32

No sooner had Ray hung up the phone, than it rang again. A now familiar voice growled through the earpiece. 'Easy bruvver.'

'Ian. I've been meaning to call you but, well, things are pretty busy.'

'Oh yeah?' Ian sounded vaguely amused. 'I see you got back all right, then.'

'Yeah. One moment.' Ray turned to Jason and made a knocking gesture on the remaining door, before walking away and leaving him to it.

'So, guess what?' Ian said.

'What's up?'

'You seen the paper today?'

'Nope, I've been pretty busy Ian. Why?'

'There's a picture on the front of the local paper. You not seen that, no?'

'The Tarnside Weekly? No, it's not really a regular read of mine.' There was a brief silence.

'John Harrington,' said Ian. He pronounced it 'Arrington'. Ray's blood ran cold for a moment. 'You know this geezer?' Ian demanded. 'Cos the paper seems to think you do, bruv.'

Ray paused for a split second, before replying coolly, 'Well, I'm CID, Ian. Obviously I know about it, yeah. Why, do you?'

'Oh yeah.' Ian paused. 'You know why he was knocked off? Do ya?' Ray was not sure how to reply. Before he could think of quite what to say, Ian continued. 'Well, look, right. I'll save you plods a bit of time. Now, it's like this, see? Harrington and this other geezer, they been bringing in these immigrants, right? Quite a lot of people getting to know about it, you get me? All sorts of erm…well…like, different sorts of people.'

'Okay,' said Ray, evenly.

'Now, you know how I feel about it, right? But me, I'm a law abiding citizen. As you know, right?' Ray said nothing. 'Right?' Ian insisted.

'I can certainly vouch for the fact you're no vigilante, Ian.'

'Right. Good. Now, Harrington has already erm…had his chips,' Ray heard Ian chuckling briefly at his own envisaged wit. 'But listen up see, there's this other geezer. Gary Brown, yeah? Now, he lives on the manor as well, right, but he ain't here just now, you get me? Word is *out*, bruv.'

'Who's looking for him?'

Ray heard Ian chuckle again. 'Nah, no chance! I'm just letting you know, init. But I think you should pick him up. Like, before you got another body to deal with.'

The phone went dead. Removing it from his ear, he looked down at it. 'Shit,' he said, just as Jason came walking up behind him.

'Another one, thinks she lived at number twenty-four. Seems to fit,' said Jason, casually. Then he saw Ray's expression. 'You all right guvnor?'

'Not really. Courtney Tumbler has just died of a heroin overdose.' Jason's jaw dropped.

'Oh my God!' he said.

'Yes. Frank is on his way over there now, he wants us to attend.'

'Shit!'

'It gets worse. We also have a man called Gary Brown running round the manor with a target on his back. Serious people are trying to kill him. Looks like the same lot who got to Harrington. It's all connected to the people trafficking, by the looks of it.' Ray put his hand to his forehead. He turned to Jason, 'This is getting out of hand. I can't do all of this on my own! Neither of us can.'

'No,' said Jason. 'But we can't act on Virtus on our own, anyway. Frank will absolutely do his nut if you charge in and bust someone to do with Virtus before you speak to him first. He made that pretty clear before.'

'You're right,' Ray replied. 'Right, well fuck this. I got better things to do than worry about a junkie whore right now. Number twenty-four, was it?'

'Yes guv.'

'I'm pretty sure I saw some suspicious behaviour in there, didn't you Detective Constable?' Ray was already walking, making his way down to the second floor.

'Well, I don't know…I…' Jason trailed behind his boss.

'Course you fucking did,' said Ray, hitting the second floor and striding aggressively down the concrete passageway. Without breaking stride, Ray raised his foot and put the door of number twenty-four through, the frame buckling with a splinter of wood. 'Go and find us some back-up, DC Stephenson. Quick!' said Ray, sarcastically. He snorted. Jason stood, uncertain of what to do. 'Go man, go. At least look like you mean it, for fuck's sake!'

'Oh right, I see. Right.' Jason disappeared to go and fetch some uniform, while Ray stood at the entrance to the flat. It was dank and gloomy. He switched on the light and immediately the scene in front of him became clear.

Whoever lived here had clearly been using for some time. Boxes of old books and magazines were scattered about the floor and piled up high against the left wall. Faded, screwed up sheets of newspaper were randomly strewn about. A filthy, green sofa lined the wall under the window and drug paraphernalia littered a small, circular table in the middle of the room. Foil, syringes, a spoon, lighters: the usual stuff. Ray walked over and looked more closely, before spying a packet of white powder. Grimacing, he nodded to himself. Almost certainly, another victim of the China White.

Ray looked through to the kitchen. Dirty plates and utensils, crusted with mouldy food, were stacked up on a filthy work surface next to the sink. On a shelf that was screwed into the right-hand wall, Ray noticed a framed photograph. The print looked old; however the glass and chrome frame were polished to a gleaming shine. It was a simple picture of a woman and a young girl, probably her daughter. Both of them were smiling, sitting in a meadow and having a picnic. Ray picked his way around the junk on the floor and picked it up. Contrasting grimly with the dusty, unloved flat in which it sat, it told its own, sad story. Ray put it back down, gently.

Jason reappeared with a Constable. Ray held both arms and palms up, to the pair of them. 'It's all right, there's nobody here, my mistake.' He pointed to the photograph. 'Looks like we've mistakenly stumbled into the home of our victim downstairs.'

'Well well well,' smirked the Constable. 'There's a slice of luck, eh?'

Chapter 33

Leaving Jason in Roe Street to secure the flat and deal with the removal of the body, Ray drove to meet Frank. When he arrived outside the colossal, black gates, he saw Frank was already waiting for him with another officer. He greeted Ray with a brief wave, got out of his car and walked over. Ray lowered the window.

'I've only just arrived myself,' Frank told them. 'Now, just let me do the talking. I've got DS Branning with me to act as the Liaison Officer for the parents, but they're not here yet. I just got word, actually, that they're currently flying in from Europe, so I don't expect them to arrive while we're here. Now, just remember, she's a celebrity. Was a celebrity.'

'Guv, I can't take any more on. I just can't,' Ray blurted out. 'Not something as high profile as this. I've just been given information on Virtus, apparently a guy called Gary Brown is currently being hunted by the same gang that took out Harrington. John Harrington wasn't a dealer, he was a people trafficker. I'm still working that murder case virtually single-handedly. Now the locals are looking to take out Brown and, judging by what happened to Harrington, there's a serious time issue here. The Detective Superintendent told me to prioritise the murder case over my other suspect on the heroin dealing, Tony Parkes, who I still want to bring in since he did a runner. We've got bodies stacking up until that gets dealt with…' Ray broke off, realizing he was imparting too much information, too quickly.

Frank put his hand to his head. 'Right. I see. You are aware that from six o' clock tonight we have twenty four hours until DI Blake is executed.'

Ray looked at him helplessly. 'I can't stop that, guv. I can only work the cases I'm assigned.' Ray tried to reason with his boss, who looked close to breaking point. 'But…well, this celebrity girl is dead, I can't help that either now. I really need to get Brown off the streets, before he joins her in the morgue.'

'Gary Brown is just a low life piece of filth!' Frank suddenly exploded on Ray. 'If he gets what's coming to him, then fuck him,' he added, savagely.

Ray was slightly taken aback, but he had also had a pretty rough day. He held his ground. 'Brown is the only lead we've got on Virtus and I don't think I'm going to get another. If we don't find him fast, the problem is only going to get worse.'

'Problem? What problem? Virtus is just some bloody, political stunt to look tough on immigration. We have absolutely no evidence of people trafficking in this division.' Frank looked at Ray and then cocked his head to one side, dangerously. He pointed a fat finger through the window, right into his face. 'You better start talking, Jackson, or I'm going to drag you out the car myself.'

'I have just been working the Virtus case, that's all. I got a lead last night and went down to the docks to check it out. I witnessed people coming in, but the group got attacked by another gang and scattered. Then they spotted me and gave chase and I narrowly escaped being hospitalised, or worse.'

'Last night?' said Frank, incredulously.

'Yes guv, last night. And I was in for five this morning. So we're both pretty tired, here.'

'Why haven't you told me about this before?'

'I just haven't had time. I've had a witness in this morning doing an ID, a meeting with the DI, I've had another body turn up which I've had to leave a DC to deal with, and it's what, two-thirty? I only got the information on Brown literally within the past hour. Now I'm here, about to go and see the body of Courtney Tumbler.' There was a brief silence.

'To be honest, I don't know a lot about her,' said Frank, his tone now more even. 'I thought maybe you could fill me in a bit.'

Ray shrugged. 'You're asking the wrong person, guv. I hate celebrities. She sings, that's all I know, the sort of cringey stuff that ten year olds go out and buy, along with their trainer bra. This is going to be a major scandal. If it's the China White that's killed her, then the best thing we can do is get that shit off the streets, fast. And I can't do that sitting here. Or in there. With all due respect, guv.'

It did not take Frank long to make a decision. 'Okay, go and get Brown and bring him in. Spin his place as well, I know him, he's bound to have something hidden in there, stolen goods, drugs, some sort of contraband. I'll sort out the authorisation for you now, then deal with this Courtney girl. And I'll speak to Paul about the priorities he has assigned you. Until then, do as he says. Leave Parkes out of it and concentrate on Virtus. How sure are you on Parkes anyway? I mean really now. No bullshit.'

'I have one witness who will *not* testify that he dealt her some H4, the homeless girl from the warehouse OD.'

'Is that all you've got?' Frank did not sound impressed.

'Yes, but I believe her, she identified him from our database in the nick, she knew his first name, the profile matches.'

'We'll never make it stick, Ray. Not without evidence. Also, if he gave you the slip, then chances are he'll have concealed any drugs by now. Forget it. Paul told you to wait until Parkes turned up, did he?'

'Yes guv. But now, this has happened.' Ray nodded towards the enormous mansion in front of them. Frank rubbed his neck.

'Well, I'm getting cramp here. Right now, I need to deal with this,' Frank motioned to the gates in front of him. 'You go and find Brown, before he gets himself killed. I'll make the necessary phone calls.'

Ray nodded, closed the window and drove away from the gates. He suspected that now the girl's parents were not going to be on the scene, Frank was probably less concerned about the number of officers he was seen to be attending with.

Once safely out of sight, Ray pulled the car over, cut the engine and dialled Ian's number. Ian answered after one ring.

'Easy bruv,' he said. 'What you after?'

'Can you talk?' said Ray.

'Yeah, what's up?'

'I'm looking for Brown.'

'Nah, I don't deal that shit.' Ian laughed.

'Seriously, where is he?'

'Seriously, where's my money man? I don't work for free. You already owe me a monkey.'

'A monkey? For nearly getting me killed?'

'Got away, din't ya? Thanks to me. Again.'

'You're the reason I was there in the first place!' Ray exclaimed.

'The info was good,' Ian countered. 'You want Brown, you pay up. That's how this game works.'

'If you give me Brown, I'll sort you the five hundred. But I need him *now*.'

'Well, don't go to his place then,' Ian laughed. 'I know for definite like, he ain't there.'

'If I find him and nick him in the next half hour, we have a deal. That's it,' Ray said. 'So give it your best guess.' There was a pause.

'Try the snooker club down the railway arches, you know it?' Ian asked.

'Yeah, I know it. If he's there, we have a deal.'

'Oh, he's there.'

'How do you know?'

Ian laughed again before replying. 'Cos I'm looking at him, bruv.'

Chapter 34

Pulling up in front of the entrance to Diamonds Snooker Centre, Ray saw the squad car he had requested was already outside, in the form of a silver Vauxhall. Both Constables would have received a picture of the suspect; however, they had been instructed not to enter the premises before Ray arrived on the scene. They had both taken a position either side of the only door and were now monitoring the people passing out of the club. Ray glanced down the street and saw a young man with a pool case approaching, head down as he strolled down the street, smoking. He saw the teenager glance up briefly. Spotting the two officers standing outside the building, the youngster suddenly decided he had somewhere else to be and turned around, swiftly walking back from the direction he had come. Ray shook his head. Sometimes it felt like the whole world had something to hide.

He exited the vehicle and took the smaller officer, a female Constable, into the building with him. Ray left the burly male officer on the door, in case Gary Brown decided to make a run for it. Two narrow flights of steps doubled over one another, before the entrance opened up into a large, rectangular snooker hall. A selection of fruit machines stood along the left-hand side, ahead of them a long bar stretched down the remaining length of the wall. To the immediate right stood a selection of pool tables with blue felt, whilst past them and through a large archway stood the larger snooker tables, evenly spaced, an array of green contrasting with the dark red walls. The hall was kept dimly lit on purpose, as long lights overhung each table, coin slots on the walls corresponding with the table numbers. Unless you wanted to play snooker in the gloom, it was useful to have a few pound coins handy.

Behind the bar stood two young women, both polishing glasses. Ray went swiftly over to the bar, flashed his identity card and informed them he was here to arrest a suspect. Before they had time to react, Ray was striding over to the back of the club where he had spied Gary Brown, bending down over the cue ball and about to take a shot.

'Gary Brown?' Ray began, holding up his identity card. 'Police. We'd like to ask you a few questions.' Gary Brown stood up from the table, looking unconcerned. He was in his mid-thirties, a slender figure with short, black hair and a square, clean shaven face.

'What?' he said.

'Not here. Down at the station.'

Gary Brown now looked slightly more concerned. 'What's this about?' he demanded.

'I think you know. Would you like to come voluntarily? The exit is also blocked, so it's up to you. I would suggest that running is not going to look good.'

Ray had nothing to formally charge Gary with at the moment. He had sent Mitchell and Rachel over to the property to conduct a search under PACE, as he did not have time to apply for a warrant from the magistrate's court. It was a gamble and not one that Ray felt terribly comfortable taking. It had all seemed quite logical on the way here, after speaking with Ian and Frank. Now, with his neck on the line, Ray was not quite so sure this had been a good idea.

'Fine,' said Gary, and began calmly unscrewing his cue. He placed the cue into its case and clipped it shut. Picking up his jacket from one of the seats along the wall, he allowed Ray to accompany him down the steps, out of the pool hall and into the squad car. Getting into the vehicle Gary looked up at Ray. 'This better be good,' he said, fiercely.

The squad car drove away as Ray walked back to his own vehicle. Starting the engine, he reflected on what he was going to say to Gary when he got back to the station. As he drove off, he looked in the rear-view mirror. He watched as Ian emerged from the snooker hall and walked off down the street, hands in his pockets, whistling.

***

Detective Constables Rachel Acorn and Mitchell Wright arrived at Brook Hill estate in an unmarked car. They pulled up behind a marked police car that contained three, uniformed Constables. Mitchell stared up at the three tower blocks, stretching up above them to the skies. Fresh graffiti had appeared on the wooden panel fencing in huge, filled, black letters. **BULLDOGS**. Alongside it was a massive swastika symbol.

'I take it this is what the guvnor was on about,' said Mitchell to his counterpart in the passenger seat. Rachel stared at the symbol and chewed her lip.

'What did he say, exactly? You took the call,' she replied.

'Not much. Gary Brown is in custody. He's suspected to be part of a trafficking ring, bringing in illegals. Apparently the locals have got wind of it and now he's not very popular.'

'I thought we're meant to be looking for drugs?'

'We're looking for anything that can keep him locked up for a while, until we can get some answers, I think,' said Mitchell. 'The guvnor also said he's got form for all sorts, but mainly dealing, so I guess he's banking on us finding something or other.' Mitchell broke off. 'I don't know, it's a bit of an odd one really. Guess we just give the place a spin and see what turns up.'

'Right,' she replied, undoing her seatbelt and putting a hand on the door latch. She looked at Mitchell. 'Let's do it.'

The three blocks were set at right angles to each other, forming a three-sided square. The nearest block to the roadside formed the central position, the length of it running parallel to the pavement where they stood. The sides of the adjacent tower blocks formed two walkways, either side. Both led into a central area, a concrete zone, overlooked on three sides by the looming buildings. The locals referred to the concrete space as the 'Pit'.

Beyond the Pit and the three tower blocks, parched grass grew in clumps over an open space that was intersected by a tarmac pathway. Originally intended as a green area, it now simply existed as a barren expanse, devoid of people or life, a dustbowl in the summer and a muddy pit for the rest of the year. It also served as a toilet for the various breeds of dog kept locally and an invisible dividing line for the gangs of teenagers that fought each other, seemingly convinced they had something worth protecting.

The council estate stretched on for some distance, the tower blocks simply forming the northeast sector. The entire area of Brook Hill was notorious; drugs an accepted part of life for the residents here, extreme violence relatively commonplace. The three tower blocks were no longer as troublesome as they once had been, since many of the occupants had been moved and the flats boarded up. Nonetheless, the few remaining tenants were still feared by most of Brook Hill, and universally hated by Tarnside as a whole.

As Mitchell and Rachel joined the three male Constables assembled on the pavement, a young kid stood watching them from high above. Wearing a grey tracksuit and matching hoodie, he pulled the hood up over his head. Then he took a large, blue handkerchief from his pocket and tied it round his face. With just his eyes now showing from behind his makeshift disguise, he hung over one of the stairwell railings and spat towards the group below. Then he bent down, picked up half a brick and took aim, carefully.

Chapter 35

SMASH! The windscreen of the squad car shattered with a tremendous noise. All five officers looked up immediately and saw the youngster, who used two arms to swear at them. Then he deliberately pulled out a small canister with a red cone on it and pointed it towards them. The deafening noise rang out over the estate as the air horn blared out its warning. The sound was comparable to the fog horns used by the ships out at sea, a noise that could be heard from time to time on Pebble Beach when the weather closed in. Then the kid disappeared. Gone.

'Chavvy little shit!' exclaimed one of the officers, looking at the damage to the vehicle.

'Right,' said Rachel, swiftly taking charge, 'now the entire estate knows we're coming, I suggest we get on with it. Saffron Court is on the left, Beech Hill House is on the right and Heather House, where we're going, is right in front of us.' Placing her back to Mitchell, she turned to the three Constables. 'One of you is going to have to stay here, guard the vehicle and get this sorted out. I expect that was the idea. Get some back-up down here if I were you.' Taking a step towards the building, she looked back over her shoulder. 'Well come on then, let's go!'

Rachel led the way to the concrete staircase at a brisk pace. She knew the estate better than Mitchell and headed straight up to the third floor of Heather House. Stairs were at either side of the blocks and the passageways were interconnected along the width of the building, from front to back, on each floor. All the flats backed onto each other and in front of all the doors ran uniform, concrete walkways, interspersed slabs of concrete and railings forming their exterior barriers.

'Sooner they demolish this place, the better,' said Mitchell as they climbed the stairs, echoing the thoughts of many an officer over the years. Nobody replied, all four of them just wanted to get in and get the job done, as fast as possible. The atmosphere was hostile and oppressive and every member of the team privately wished they were somewhere else.

As they got to the second floor, they heard calling, laughing and shouting from high above, unmistakably youngsters. 'It's the fuckin' old bill, init.' Another young voice hollered down from above, 'OI! CUNT FLAPS!'

Rachel turned to Mitchell, directly behind her on the stairway. 'I take it that was meant for me. These fellas certainly know how to flatter a girl!' Her joke broke the tension a little and all the male officers laughed. The Constable behind Mitchell spoke quietly in his ear.

'Got some bottle, hasn't she?' he said, admiringly.

'Hmm,' said Mitchell. 'Let's hope so.'

'Nah, she has,' said the other uniform, who was at the back. 'She worked with vice down here for ages. She doesn't give a fuck, believe it.'

Rachel stomped up to number 341 and rapped on the wooden door. A woman in her late twenties opened it, her blonde hair scraped back behind her head in a tight, high ponytail, oily skin peppered with acne. Rachel pushed inside. 'Police, stand back please.'

'OI, you can't come in 'ere,' the woman protested. 'I got kids in 'ere, OI.' The men pushed inside. 'What you DOING?'

'We believe there may be controlled substances on the premises,' said Rachel.

'You better 'av a warrant!' the woman threatened.

'We don't need one, welcome to the twenty-first century,' Rachel snarled back. 'Gary's down the nick, now you gonna show me? Or am I gonna have to rip your children's bedrooms into pieces?'

'You fuckin' little bitch!' the woman screamed at her. A baby started crying and a little girl ran into the kitchen, a finger in her mouth.

'Yeah, yeah,' said Rachel, getting right in the woman's face. She held it for a moment, eyes wide, aggressive, nodding slightly. Then she stepped back. 'Right boys, let's get to work. Turn this hole upside down.'

The three officers immediately began opening cupboards and emptying the contents onto the floor. Cans, biscuits, fruit, cereals.

'I am gonna fuckin' 'av you for this,' the woman yelled, her eyes flashing as she stood, pointing at Rachel. She turned and ushered her daughter back into the sitting room, her hand on the back of the child's head. The baby started to scream.

Mitchell stood and kept still for a moment. All the cupboards were now open and he scanned around. He did a complete circle, then looked up towards the ceiling. Spotting a small, circular biscuit tin on top of one of the kitchen cupboards, he retrieved it and tried to remove the lid. It would not budge. Rachel held out her hand. 'You shouldn't bite your nails,' she said, nodding at his hands. She levered hers under the lid and twisted, managing to free it. Looking at the contents, she smiled. She passed it back to Mitchell so he could look inside. Then he smiled too.

At that moment, the woman came back into the kitchen, holding a baby that had a face streaked with tears. Rachel held up the tin. 'Baking, are we?'

***

Ray received the news literally minutes before he was due to speak with Gary Brown. It rocked him.

'China White?' Ray said into the telephone. 'China White?'

'Looks like it, guv. It could be something else I suppose. I'm not really inclined to stick my finger in and find out,' Rachel replied.

'No, don't. The stuff is lethal, seriously. You'd be high as a kite just from a sniff of the stuff.'

'Well, yes, guv.' Rachel's tone was flat.

'You know what I mean,' said Ray. 'Look, please get it back here immediately, okay? Leave Mitchell and the other Constables to finish the search. I have Gary here, I'm literally about to go into the interview room.'

'Okay guv, I'll do that now,' she replied. 'We can test it using EDIT, right?'

'Yes, that's right. If I'm not available, make sure the test is done by a trained tester, ask the Skipper whose available. In fact, I'll do it before you get here. Just report to the Duty Sergeant. Tell him I want the MG11 an hour ago.'

'I'll have the form filled out as soon as the test is done and we've confirmed what this is. I'll bring it straight to you.'

'Great, I'll be in Interview Room Three. With our friend here. See you very soon.' Ray hung up the phone and went to the Duty Sergeant, briefly explained the situation and the returned to the interview room. He opened the door.

'Hello Gary,' Ray said.

'What's this all about?'

Ray sat down in the bare room, which contained just a table and three chairs. 'How well did you know John Harrington, Gary?'

'Oh right, yeah.' Gary looked relieved. 'I saw that in the paper today. Dreadful business, that. Shocking.' He looked down and shook his head.

'Know him well, did you?' Ray asked.

'Oh yeah, well, you know. Live on the same manor.'

'So you did know him well?'

'Oh no, not now. I used to, but not really close nowadays. No idea why anyone would have wanted to hurt old Harris. I'm guessing that's what this is all about?'

'It looks like you're up to your neck in all sorts of things, Gary. Right now, I'm hoping you're going to tell me all about the little human trafficking ring you had going on with Harrington.'

'You what, mate?' Then he laughed. 'Do *what*? I think you've got the wrong geezer pal. I don't know what you're talking about. I really don't.'

'I guess you don't know anything about the heroin in your flat, either?' Ray enquired, coolly. Gary's face changed fast, from mocking, to disbelief, then swiftly to anger.

'No I certainly don't,' he said, with feeling. 'Certainly wouldn't have that shit in my house.' Gary paused, clearly getting angry. 'You want to fit me up, do you? That it? Well, I'm not here under caution, you know. I ain't done nothing wrong.' Gary waved his hand dismissively and gathered his jacket from the back of his seat. 'See you later.' Gary pointed at Ray. 'You're a fucking plank, mate.' He rose from his seat behind the table.

'This is your last chance to co-operate, Gary. Tell me about Harrington and your little trafficking ring and I might be able to help you out.'

'Go to hell,' said Gary. 'You've got nothing on me.'

'Gary Brown, I am arresting you on suspicion of possession with intent to supply a Class A substance, you do not have to say anything but it may harm your defence if you do not mention when questioned something which you later rely on in court. Anything you do say may be given in evidence.'

Chapter 36

Ray looked at his phone. The time read six o' clock. Twenty-four hours until DI Blake was allegedly set to meet her maker. Gary Brown was refusing to say another word until he spoke to a solicitor and Ray was now starving. Then he remembered Ellie. He had given her thirty quid to get something clean to wear and he had also given her the spare key to his house, figuring that if she wanted to rob him she would have done it already. Either that, or she would just take the money and be gone, but Ray wanted to give that option. Let her make her own choices and live with them. When he had given her the key and the money, she had smiled slightly and thanked him and then promised to do him dinner. For six o'clock.

Ray rang his home phone but nobody picked up. He would have left a message, but his answerphone service was provided by the phone network; therefore, unlike some of the old machines that plug into the wall, when someone was leaving a message it was not audible. With Gary under arrest in a cell and still awaiting the results from the EDIT, Ray left the office and sped home. He was back by quarter past six.

'Sorry, I'm a bit late,' he said, walking through the front door in a rush. Ellie stood at the hob and something smelt quite good. Putting his keys down, Ray noticed something looked quite good as well.

'Hello,' she said, turning to face him. She looked quite different, again. 'I went shopping,' she said. Ray didn't know quite what to say.

Ellie had always been hidden since he had first laid eyes on her, either under a duvet or under a jumble of baggy clothes, frequently smelly ones. Ray had not thought much about it – until now.

In the first instance, she had sorted her hair out, which must have taken a considerable length of time. Ray thought she had managed to do a fairly good job of it. The matted part was cut out and it was now gathered to one side in a loose ponytail. Her light, blonde hair also had some body and shone for the first time since Ray had met her, accentuating her dark, blue eyes.

She was sporting a tight, black cotton top over a new bra, supporting a modest bust. The top reached down to her belly button, which was pierced with a belly bar. Her waist was visible for the first time ever and it was tight, leading down to a shapely backside and two long, slender legs, all outlined by a skin-tight pair of dark blue, denim jeans.

'Wow,' said Ray. 'You look great.' She blushed and turned away, back to the hob. Something shifted in their relationship for Ray in that moment. She did not look like a lost little girl anymore, not at all. She looked every bit her age, a young woman who was nearly twenty. He poured himself a whisky. Once more, she had completely thrown him.

'So,' said Ray. 'What's your full name, I don't even know.'

'Ah,' said Ellie. 'I was wondering when you would ask me that. Eleanor Bradshaw.'

'Nice,' he replied, glancing at her again, as she stood with her back to him. She looked amazing, he could barely believe she was standing in his kitchen, making him dinner. Ray did not know quite what to say, it was like meeting her for the first time, all over again. He felt flustered. He drank his drink.

'Nice name, you mean?' she said, turning around with a wooden spoon in her hand.

'Yes,' he replied. 'Nice name.' She stood there, looking at him. Then she smiled and licked the spoon.

'Thanks,' she said, turning around again. Ray swallowed.

'So, what's for dinner?' he asked.

'Just bolognaise. I can't cook anything else,' she said, bluntly. 'So how was your day? Pretty long, huh? I had a sleep this afternoon. I slept on your bed, hope you don't mind.'

'No,' said Ray.

'It's very comfortable,' she said. 'Oh, I bought a bit of make-up as well, but it's amazing how much you can pick up for free. I got loads of stuff.'

'You didn't nick it, did you?' Ray asked, suddenly alarmed.

'No,' she laughed. 'I meant testers. Like free stuff, you know. Promos and that.'

'Oh right. What, they just give stuff away?' Ray said, doubtfully.

'Yep,' she said. Turning back to him and seeing the look on his face, she added, 'Oh, you're a bloke, you wouldn't understand!'

'Well, you don't need make-up anyway, you look great just as you are,' Ray replied, before realizing that could be taken a number of different ways and he was not sure he had meant to imply any of them. 'Not that I meant, you know, I minded. Or that, well, you know…'

'Hmmm?' she said.

Ray downed his drink. 'I have a habit of saying the wrong thing at the wrong time, don't worry. It's fairly standard,' he said, by means of explanation.

'Oh, I don't mind,' Ellie replied. She paused, before stating simply, 'I stammer sometimes.'

'Do you?' Ray was genuinely surprised. 'I never knew that.'

'Only when I feel scared or something,' she said, turning to look at him again. 'When I can't, I mean, I don't, have time to think…' She trailed off still looking at him and started to smile again. 'I don't think that's ever happened with you though.'

***

A mobile phone in the Incident Room dealing with the abduction of Rosie Blake started to ring. Paul grabbed the arm of his superior officer. Albert drew back a step, about to admonish him, wondering what the hell had got into the Detective Superintendent; before in a flash, he realized what was happening. Paul just stood there for a second, clutching his arm, before he realized what he was doing and let go. Nothing was said. Albert looked at Paul and the two men stared at each other for a few, dreadful seconds.

'Tomorrow?' Paul's voice was almost a whisper. 'That was right, wasn't it, guv?'

'Yes,' replied Albert. Then he seized the phone and answered it. 'Detective Chief Superintendent Manson speaking.'

In less than a minute, the call was over. The Detective Chief Superintendent turned to Paul and started to grin, which for Albert was a rare thing.

'It seems one of our lads has struck gold,' he said. Then the colour paled slightly from his face. 'We are holding a Gary Brown downstairs, aren't we?'

'I don't know guv. I can check with the Duty Sergeant. Why?'

'Well, we'd better be. The people holding Blake…they want to do an exchange.'

Chapter 37

Ray and Ellie were both sitting on the sofa opposite the mute television, each with a plate of spaghetti bolognaise on a tray. Neither of them were watching the twenty-four hour news channel that Ray had switched on, a habitual practice when he got home. The bolognaise was tasty and the pair of them were hungry. Ray, in particular, was concentrating solely on the food in front of him.

'Oh my God!' said Ellie, suddenly. 'Can you turn it up?' Ray glanced up to the television and grimaced. That had not taken long. He unmuted the volume.

'...found this afternoon, died of a suspected heroin overdose. Police however, are refusing to comment on the exact cause of death until the results of the post-mortem have been received. Courtney Tumbler was not known to have been a regular drug user and her death has shocked her fans and the wider community she worked within, many of whom are struggling to come to terms with what has happened today.

'The death also coincides with a spate of recent overdose victims within the Tarnside vicinity. Our sources suggest that a strain of the drug, far exceeding the twenty-six percent purity usually found at street level, is rapidly becoming widely available...'

Ray turned it off. Ellie looked at him, 'Hey, I was watching that!' Ray looked back at her.

'Well, there's not much more to tell. I just want to switch off for a bit.' He sighed.

'Oh,' Ellie said, 'I see. Not news to you then, huh?'

'Not when it happens on our ground, no. I was there this afternoon. After I'd been down Roe Street and picked up another dead hooker.' Ray felt exhausted and he sat back in his seat, closing his eyes.

Ellie looked over. 'Is your job always like this?'

Ray did not reply, he was not sure what to say. There was a silence.

'Is this what happened with your last girlfriend?' Ellie asked.

'What?' he said, irritably. 'Did what happen?'

'Sometimes you just don't answer things, that's all. You just ignore me. And you seem to work all the time. Is that why she left you?'

Ray did not trust himself to reply. Images of the dead woman he had seen earlier kept flashing through his head for some reason: the vomit on the concrete, the strange angles of her legs, the photograph on her shelf. He was too tired to cope with all these questions. His personal life was not something he talked about. Ever.

'I don't know,' he snapped. 'Probably. Maybe that's why she immediately went and fucked my best friend, you'd have to ask her.' The recollection and the admission made him feel angry and humiliated. He looked daggers at her and she looked away, frightened. 'Happy?' he said, nastily.

'Sorry, I didn't m...m...m...' Then she pushed her plate to the floor and ran upstairs and Ray knew she was going to cry. He stood up, simultaneously upset and angry at himself for the situation he had caused.

'You see,' he called up the stairs, angrily, 'this is exactly what happened. It's just ME. I'm just a complete, fucking, arsehole.' Then he snatched up his keys and left the house, slamming the door.

Walking down the street, Ray felt his stomach churning, a mass of memories and conflicting emotions clouding his vision. At that moment, his mobile phone rang. 'Yes,' Ray snapped as he answered.

'Ray, it's Frank. I'm just letting you know, we've got a bit of a situation involving the prisoner, Gary Brown.'

'Right,' said Ray, struggling to control his voice. 'What's the situation?'

'The people holding Rosie Blake telephoned this evening. They want to do an exchange for Brown. Also, there could potentially be a slight problem on the warrant.'

Ray sighed heavily. 'I thought that was sorted out, guv.'

'Yes, well it's probably fine. It's just that he was charged after the stuff was found and there was a woman at the property when Wright and Acorn arrived on scene. It's possible that the Brief might have a case on the time lag.'

'We basically busted in and ripped the place apart without a warrant and before we had officially made an arrest,' Ray summarised.

'Yes,' Frank replied. 'I thought you were going to arrest him, I didn't realize you were going to bring him in for chat.' Frank's voice was flat, there was no blame implied.

'Sorry, I've fucked things up again,' said Ray, miserably.

'It's okay, in fact, as it turns out, it's fine,' said Frank. 'Gary doesn't know yet, he thinks he's looking at a long stretch. And we found about twenty grand's worth of that China White. Ray, it's a good result.' Frank paused for a moment, before continuing. 'Anyway, Paul had a little chat with Gary since you left the station. The upshot of it all is, Gary seems to think walking out of here with his liberty is a good idea. So, we *are* going to do the swap. I thought you would want to know the situation. Are you all right, Ray? You sound a bit upset?'

'I've just upset my...friend,' Ray replied, awkwardly. There was a silence.

'You're not gay, are you?' Frank sounded incredulous.

'No, I'm not gay,' Ray replied, irritably. 'Why does everyone keep asking me that?'

'Oh, right.' Frank sounded relieved. 'No reason. I didn't know you were seeing anyone. Why don't you just call her your girlfriend? Oh, never mind, it's well beyond me, your generation. Look, if you want to be there, we're leaving the station at nine tonight, it's a big operation and the Firearms Unit are involved as well.' Frank paused. 'You don't need to be there Ray, I know you've had a long couple of days. I can't tell you the location at the moment, obviously. Why don't you sort things out with your... your friend, and see how you feel. All right?'

'Thanks guv. I'll be there.'

'Good man. See you tonight.'

Frank hung up. Ray returned back to the house, Frank's voice still ringing in his ears. *Why don't you just call her your girlfriend?*

'For fuck's sake, Frank,' said Ray, out loud as he walked straight back to his house. He entered quietly and gently closed the front door. Ellie was in the sitting room, head down, clearing up the dinner she had spilt. Ray walked over to her, took her hand and lifted her up to a standing position, opposite him.

'I'm really sorry,' he said. She stood there, tearful, and he could see she was afraid of him. He put his hand up to her face, gently, and pushed her hair back. She was actually trembling, which shook him quite a bit. 'I…I don't know what's happened to you before; but I would never, ever, hurt you. Not ever,' Ray told her.

She put both hands on his chest and pushed him away. 'I only asked you a question,' she said. 'You looked like you were gonna kill me. What the fuck is the matter with you, hmm?' Her voice quivered slightly. Then, without warning, she completely broke down.

With a dreadful wail she collapsed down onto the sofa and began sobbing violently, her breath coming in gasps. She held both her hands over her face as tears poured down her cheeks. 'You're all the same,' she cried, before pulling her knees up to her body and wrapping her arms around them, defensively. Burying her face in her knees she sat there, gasping, rocking gently, whilst endless streams of tears poured out from somewhere deep inside.

Witnessing the depth of her misery, Ray was appalled. 'We're not all the same,' he said, trying to sound calm. 'I don't hit women for a start.' Ray felt his jaw clench. 'Did someone hit you in the past?' Anger burnt up through his face. He sat down quickly on the sofa alongside her, concerned his expression might frighten her again.

Ellie kept her face buried in her knees, her sobbing lessening as she brought herself back under control. Still hiding behind her hair, she just nodded a few times.

'Who?' Ray demanded.

She shook her head back and looked straight at him, her chin up. Her face was bright red, soaked with tears and snot, her make-up had run and strands of her pretty, golden hair were stuck across her face. 'Everybody,' she gasped. 'Everybody hits me. Because I'm stupid.'

Chapter 38

Ray took one look at Ellie and simply did what came naturally. He gathered her up in his arms and cuddled her, stroking her hair and kissing the top of her head. After a couple of minutes, she had calmed down. Gathering her breath back, she unwrapped herself, dropping her knees to the floor. Ray stood and went to the kitchen area, ripping some paper towel off the roll and bringing it over to her.

'I really am sorry,' he said. He felt dreadful. She shook her head, took the tissues and blew her nose. Wiping her face, she pulled herself together.

'It's not your fault,' she said, looking at the floor. 'I shouldn't have asked such a stupid question.' This only made Ray feel worse.

'You can ask me whatever you like,' he said. 'I just...' Ray broke off, unsure of himself or what to say.

'I thought that, maybe, if you talked about it, you would get over it. I'm sorry,' she said and started to cry again.

'I am over it, believe me. It just makes me angry remembering, that's all. I don't really talk about it.' Ray stopped.

'You don't have to,' she said. 'But...' she trailed off. She blew her nose and stopped crying.

'Tell me,' he said.

'You won't like it,' she replied. She shook her head.

'Honestly, I would rather you asked me. I really would,' he added, with feeling.

'How long ago was it? That you broke up?' Ellie looked over at him, a rabbit in the headlights. Ray exhaled, heavily.

'Six years ago,' he said.

Ellie nodded, looking at the floor. 'That's a long time, Ray. A long time ago.'

'Yeah.' He wanted to wanted to add something flippant: that it was no big deal, that he had got over it years ago. But something stopped him from lying to her. 'You're right,' he said. 'It was a long time ago.'

'Six years ago I was thirteen years old. Now I'm nearly twenty. A lot of stuff has happened to me since then. But…what about you?'

Ray felt his eyes getting hot. He turned away from her. After a minute, he managed a reply. 'Not much,' he said, stiffly.

He felt her hand on his leg, comforting him. The first time a woman had comforted him in six years. 'I don't think you're stupid,' he blurted out.

She put her hand on his cheek and turned his face towards her. Then she kissed him.

***

The car-park resembled a military base camp. It appeared that every conceivable division of the police force wanted a piece of the action. The mass of officers that had been crammed into the Incident Room upstairs were now swelled by far greater numbers. The Anti-Kidnap & Extortion Unit had brought in their specialist negotiators, additional units had arrived from the Covert Policing Branch, all the officers and staff from the Cultural and Community Resource Unit were milling about, a mass of uniform were present in full riot gear and most of CID had also attended. Various teams from SOCA were on hand, most notably the Firearms Unit, which comprised the Specialist Firearms Officers, or SFOs and the Armed Response Vehicle unit, known as the ARVs.

The SFOs were stood about at the rear of the car-park, laughing and joking, holding a brutal assortment of weaponry. All of them had a Glock 17 pistol, each packing a seventeen round magazine. Six men held MP5 sub machine guns augmented with torches attached to the fore grip, four more held HK G3k assault rifles fitted with differing attachments, two with telescopic scopes for sniper work, the other pair fitted with an ergonomic stock from a PSG1, devastating in close range encounters. Two men in the SFO unit carried Benelli M3 Super 90 shotguns, loaded with 12-gauge buck-shot. All twelve of the men wore a C100 ceramic helmet, full Kevlar body armour and an assault vest packed with stun grenades, tear gas canisters and magazine pouches.

The ARVs consisted of two Jankel, Guardian MRV units: purpose-built, 4 x 4, armoured, counter-terrorist and hostage rescue intervention vehicles. These powerful machines consist of an armoured, boxed rear end, tacked onto an enormous engine and bulletproof windshield at the front. As a result of their impregnable exteriors, they are also occasionally employed for high-risk prisoner transportation.

Having parked outside, Ray walked through the main reception and made his way through the station to find his colleagues. After kissing him passionately, briefly, Ellie had pulled away. When he had gone to kiss her again, she did not seem sure at all. Then he had told her that he needed to go out tonight. She nodded and smiled, but her eyes told a different story.

Ray knew it was a well-known cliché that the police force had the highest divorce rate of any profession in the UK and that there was a good reason for that. Very few relationships could handle the strain that the job put upon it. It was not just the anti-social hours and the long days, it was also the mental state in which it left the person involved in the work. The job, by its very nature, involved witnessing horrific things, creating a whole memory bank of appalling images that was constantly added to over the years. In time, they started to blot out the happy times, crowding into the psyche unexpectedly and uninvited. Maybe by the Christmas tree, unwrapping presents with the family, or, more frequently, in bed. The effort of constantly pushing them away, of dealing with the haunting images of so many butchered corpses, of constantly plumbing the depths of human depravity and evil; it was too much for most people to handle and their relationship was often the first casualty. Everybody in the job knew it had caused many officers to end their lives completely, incapable of handling the ceaseless torment that their internal, mental recorders endlessly replayed for them. Others kept drinking, frequently, to blot the memories out and alcoholism remains rife amongst the police force.

Ray thought about Ellie constantly as he walked down the corridor towards the car-park, having parked down the road from the station. As he contemplated the evenings events, he tried to juggle his own feelings with his genuine desire to help her get back on her feet. His emotions were clouding his objectivity. He did not want to take advantage of her, or feel that he was. That had never been his intention. But he could not help how he felt now and he was suddenly thinking about her all the time. He tried to push her from his mind. The notion of them being together was ridiculous, he barely knew the girl, she was far too young anyway. Their backgrounds were completely incompatible – or were they, he wondered. She spoke quite well, not like the kids off the estate. He wondered what her background really was. Then he realized he did not really care that much. He liked her. Yes, he did like her.

'RAY!' Ray looked up and saw Frank standing at the end of the corridor.

'Guv! Sorry, miles away.'

'I see that.' Frank smiled. 'Come on Romeo, I need to brief you all. Hurry up!'

Chapter 39

Ray cut the engine and Jason, Mitchell and Rachel climbed out of the vehicle. Taking a deep breath, he undid his seat belt and followed.

The night was still and clear. It had come as no surprise to Ray that the secret location was the old dockyard. It was the most logical place he could think of for a hostage transfer. Vast, deserted, with a mixture of places for concealment and too many exit routes to effectively cover, it seemed an obvious choice. Ray had told Frank that he expected them to come in by boat, to the slipway where he had witnessed them before. Surprised at his insight, Frank had confirmed that this was, indeed, the arrangement.

'We're not trying to stop them, not tonight. We just want Rosie Blake back, in one piece. That is the priority,' Frank had confided in him at the police station.

'We're not going to give chase? Or track them with a chopper?' Ray was indignant.

'No,' came the blunt reply. 'There's a multitude of reasons. One being there is nothing to stop them doing this again and, if we have no precedent for establishing trust, then next time we might not get this opportunity.'

Ray had not trusted himself to reply immediately. On reflection, he knew it was not Frank's call, therefore arguing the toss with him about the decision to let these thugs walk would be a futile exercise. Ray stood silently for a moment, before he suspected Frank privately felt the same as he did.

'Right, guv. Understood,' he had replied. Frank had glanced at him and nodded.

Ray now trudged across the wet concrete, side-stepping enormous puddles that concealed a wealth of depressions and potential ankle-busters. The two ARV units were positioned about thirty yards apart, both vehicles parked at forty-five degree angles and about fifty yards back from the lip of the enormous slipway. It was high tide and the waves were splashing gently onto the concrete slope, still a good fifteen feet below the top of the slipway itself. The SFO teams were in position, five men with each ARV, two in the centre and three on the flanks. Ray knew the two sniper men would be concealed somewhere nearby, probably on top of different buildings or somewhere else high up, both equipped with long-range, night vision scopes.

Some distance behind the SFO units stood a plethora of uniformed officers, in full riot gear and holding a wall of shields. On each flank more of them were visible, lined up like soldiers in rows of six by three. In total, Ray estimated about sixty uniformed officers were present as a back-up. He wondered if it was really necessary, especially considering the twelve SFOs, combined with the two ARV units, held enough weaponry and firepower between them to put down a small army.

Ray was positioned with the rest of CID, well away from the action and sheltered in a disused building on the right, behind one flank of uniformed officers. He felt strangely unexcited and disengaged from the whole proceedings. He wondered why he felt like that tonight. Normally, he would have felt completely the opposite way. It crossed his mind that it had actually been a lot more exciting last time he had been here, with Ian Grant. Desperately tired, Ray rubbed his eyes and yawned. He wondered what Ellie was doing. Then he thought how nice it would be if he were watching a film right now, maybe in bed. Maybe with Ellie. Maybe in bed with Ellie. He thought back to how she had looked from behind, cooking dinner. Gorgeous.

'Ray!' A voice hissed in his ear.

'Hmm?' he said. He turned to see Jason pointing excitedly at the sea.

'Look,' Jason said.

A small speedboat was rapidly approaching, the humming noise rapidly increasing to a buzzing, before it was clearly distinguishable as the roar of two, enormous, outboard engines. In the front of the boat, hanging onto the railings, the silhouette of a figure kept bobbing up intermittently, briefly visible on the sky line as the boat skimmed over the crest of another wave, before being lost as it plunged briefly into another ocean trough.

The report came clearly through the digital radio. 'Papa Zulu two six five confirm that is Detective Inspector Rosie Blake. Advise all units standby to proceed, over.' Clearly, one of the snipers had a good view.

The boat slowed, the driver keeping well down. He appeared to be alone. The small vessel remained head on to their position. A loud hailer rang out from the ocean.

'We are ready to proceed,' came a clipped, male voice. The man did not shout and from their vantage point Ray, and the rest of the CID team, struggled to hear what was being said. They collectively held their breath. 'Bring Gary Brown forward to the dockside and we will release the woman.'

There was an eerie silence. Ray watched as Gary Brown was brought out, unbound, from the ARV parked to the left.

'Let her go and we will release the prisoner. You have our word,' said the SOCA negotiator, also equipped with a loud hailer.

It was tense stand-off for about twenty seconds. Then the voice rang out again. 'We are not armed. Just send him forward to the top of the slipway.'

'Release the woman,' came the reply. 'They need to pass each other for this to work. At the same time.'

There was another brief pause.

'Okay. We will let her swim ashore. When you see her swimming, you tell him to start walking. Otherwise we go and pick her up again. Clear?'

'Clear,' came the response.

Unable to see clearly, Ray heard a faint splash and presumed that Rosie Blake was swimming as fast as her little legs could propel her along. Legs, thought Ray. Ellie had nice legs. Nice shape to them. He exhaled. This was all rather predictably boring. Hopefully it would be over soon. Ray let a huge yawn rip. Other members of CID gave him strange looks, clearly watching the unfolding proceedings on tenterhooks.

Ray watched as Rosie reached the shore and flashlights lit her up. Watching Gary Brown walking towards the ocean, a flash of anger passed through his mind. Nobody had even mentioned the fact his prisoner, his capture, was the reason this was all going on. Ray sighed again. Another bodged arrest, another scumbag laughing at the law, walking to freedom...

TCHOOM.
Gary Brown dropped to the ground and all hell broke loose.

Chapter 40

The sound was unmistakable. Everybody present immediately realized a silenced, sniper rifle had just dropped Gary Brown with a single shot. Instant death.

'You motherfuckers!' came a furious, muffled shout from the speedboat and everyone watched Rosie Blake instantly start running up the slipway, her back curved, chest out, arms pumping, sprinting barefoot, running for her life. She travelled like a puck on an ice rink, a blur of black and white flashing across the expanse of concrete in front of her. Simultaneously, the armed SFO units advanced at a run and machine gun fire erupted from the speedboat, smashing up the concrete where Rosie had been just seconds before.

TCHOOM.

The sickening sound came again from an unseen vantage point and one of the advancing men on the left SFO unit went down, clutching his leg.

Rosie Blake was almost behind the right SFO unit and Ray heard one of the team shout at her, 'Get down, get down, down on the ground, DO it, NOW.' As they watched her obey, an armed officer ran and stood over the Detective Inspector, crouching down as the other four surrounded her, forming a defensive shield of armed police.

The speedboat roared into life as six MP5 sub machine guns illuminated its position, all opening fire and two sniper rifles rang out clearly, almost as one noise. Despite this, the boat roared off with one engine smoking, still firing back wildly as it disappeared out to sea.

'Take cover, all units!' came a loud command, triggering all the uniformed officers to break ranks and start heading for the nearest building they could find, a mass of disorganisation and blind panic.

TCHOOM.

A cry followed the noise and another SFO man on the left flanking team was hit. Then another shot rang out, clearly, high up in the sky. Ray glanced upwards and saw the mystery figure. He had been lodged into a nook in a disused, broken crane that had once been used to lift the ships from the water for anti-fouling and general maintenance. Ray watched as the figure clung on with one arm, desperately. Another shot rang out and the figure fell, tumbling, down, down and hitting the ground like a sack of maize. A dull thud.

Within seconds, a calm voice came over the airwaves. 'Papa Zulu two six five, confirm that the area is now clear, repeat, the area is now contained, over.'

'Good shooting two six five, great spot,' someone replied, presumably the head of the Firearms Unit brigade. 'Take care on the way down. Over and out.'

***

Ray arrived home well after midnight. Walking in, he immediately sat on the sofa, took off his shoes, threw his keys onto the coffee table and went straight upstairs. Exhausted, he entered his room and sat down on the edge of the bed. He had rarely felt so tired. He switched on the bedside lamp and took his shirt off, throwing it onto the floor. Then he heard a strange, whistling noise.

Turning around, he saw Ellie was fast asleep on the other side of his double bed, almost completely buried under the duvet. He was so tired that his first reaction was almost one of annoyance, before he reflected this was actually a pretty good result. His thoughts then wandered as to what she might be wearing. He yawned again and put a hand to his head. Desperately tired, he was beyond caring what she might be wearing right now. He leant over and kissed her cheek, took his trousers and socks off and climbed into bed in his boxer shorts. Within three minutes, Ray was fast asleep.

When he woke up, sunlight was streaming through the window. Blinking, he turned to his left but Ellie was not there. He lay back, unsure of what this meant. Then he looked at the clock, realized it was quarter to eleven and that he had just slept solidly for more than ten hours. Little wonder then, she had got out of bed.

He pulled some jeans on and went into the bathroom. He heard the television on downstairs. After a quick wash, he ambled down the stairway and into the sitting room.

'Morning,' he said.

'Hello,' said Ellie. 'You slept a long time.'

'Yeah,' he said. 'Needed it. You been up long?'

'Nope,' she said.

Ray walked past the back of the sofa into the kitchen. 'You want a cup of tea?' he asked.

'Thanks,' she said, holding a mug up.

Turning around, he saw she wasn't wearing much. A pair of hot pants and a T-shirt, sitting with her legs folded up to her chest again, watching the television.

'I saw you fell asleep in my bed last night,' he said.

She giggled. 'I told you, it's very comfortable,' she replied. Ray did not know what to say. Half of him felt he should back right off, the other half wanted to jump right in. Torn, he confronted her.

'Have you many boyfriends, then?' he asked, busying himself by filling the kettle. 'Seeing as you wanted to know all about my love life, I think I have a right to know where *you've* been.' Immediately, Ray realized how that had come out. 'I mean, not like that, you know. Just a figure of speech.'

Ellie raised her eyebrows. 'Not one I've heard before,' she replied. 'Anyway,' she continued, 'I haven't been anywhere. In fact, as you ask, I'm still on the forecourt.'

'Oh yeah?' said Ray, smiling.

'Yes,' she said, seriously. 'Never even been out for a test drive.' Then Ray realized what she was telling him.

'Oh right,' he said, still half laughing, but not quite sure if he should be. 'Really? You're pulling my leg?'

She shook her head. 'No. I'm not.' She smiled sweetly and went back to watching the television.

'But...you must have had boyfriends before?' Ray pushed her.

'Not really. Had more important things to worry about. Like getting high and going clubbing and sometimes just finding a place to crash without some pervert trying to stick his hand up my skirt.' She did not take her eyes off the television.

'Oh. Right.' Again, not an answer he had expected. Her ability to constantly surprise him continued unabated.

'I don't see why you're quite so surprised,' she said, sounding mildly offended. 'Do I look like some sort of slapper?'

'No!' Ray exclaimed. He came and sat down on the sofa, casually. 'Just thought that, well, given your age, you might have…you know…before.'

She looked at him again, her big eyes holding his for a moment. 'No,' she said calmly, a measured response. 'I just wasn't ready and then I just wasn't with the right person. All right?'

'Yep,' Ray said. There was an awkward silence. 'I just wondered,' he added. She nodded once and the conversation was over.

'Just one other thing I was wondering,' Ray said, determined to get some answers before something happened he might live to regret. She turned and faced him. Then she started to smile, wryly.

'No, I've never stuck a needle in myself, either. Not that I can imagine why you would want to know. Shall we change the subject?'

'Oh no, I wasn't going to ask that,' he lied.

Chapter 41

Rosie was sitting in the office of Detective Chief Superintendent Manson, along with Paul and Frank. She had told them everything that had occurred and she had nothing more to add. Despite this, the three men seemed unwilling to allow her to return to work.

'I really think you should take a few days off, at least,' Albert was saying. 'The shock and trauma, I mean, you nearly got killed last night. We have two SFOs in hospital with bullets in their legs, one is lucky that he'll ever walk again. One inch higher and his whole kneecap would have been blown away. Under the circumstances, I re…'

'Sir, with all due respect, I have sat about doing very little for days on end, I am unhurt and have no desire to sit around at home, on my own, for the foreseeable future. It does not appeal to me. Nor do I feel like a holiday, just at the moment.' Rosie was always professional, but never afraid to put her point across.

'I don't really understand any of it,' Paul butted in. 'I just don't. Why did they kidnap you, for a start? You weren't even on Virtus, we put a DS on that. And why did they take out Brown? It certainly wasn't one of our boys. It makes no sense at all to me.' He regarded her with a look that bordered on the suspicious.

'Brown and Harrington were involved in people smuggling,' Frank interjected. 'We pulled Brown in because Brook Hill got wind of it and some of the racist scum up there were looking to take him out. My guess is one of them got wind of the transfer arrangements and took their opportunity.'

'Well, now I've heard it all,' said Paul, sarcastically. 'Not only did they know exactly when the transfer was taking place, they also had a hit marksman on hand, with a night scoped, silenced, long range sniper rifle to take him out. Fuck me, they've moved up in the world. And there's me, thinking it's a bunch of chavs hanging about on an estate set for demolition.' Paul looked around the room and saw everybody looking at him. 'Sorry,' he said. 'That was uncalled for.'

Albert cleared his throat. 'It was; however, you do make a fair point. I can't understand any of it either. I am, genuinely, delighted that you are safe Rosie. That was always the priority here, I made that absolutely clear to everyone involved.' Albert put his hands behind his back and took a few paces across the room. He stopped at the window and looked out on the world below. 'I don't know where the rogue shooter came from last night. Or why he was there. However, I have a feeling that it might well have stirred up a hornets' nest.' He turned and faced the group, grimly. 'I don't think this is over.'

***

'So,' Ellie said, 'You not going to work today?'

'We had a pretty eventful night,' Ray replied. He told her what had happened the previous evening and she listened with growing excitement, her eyes growing wider as he described the blaze of gun fire. When he had finished, however, she just looked confused.

'So why did he get shot?'

'Nobody knows.'

'That doesn't make sense. I thought they wanted him freed. Otherwise they wouldn't have released the woman?'

'Gary Brown was involved in the people smuggling ring I told you about before. Down at the docks, when I got chased. He was working with that bloke in the paper this week. John Harrington?'

Ellie's face changed. 'Harris?'

That shook Ray slightly. 'You knew him then, did you?'

'Yes, I knew Harris. He was the dealer I most used to score tar off, when I picked up for Mike.' She looked away from him. 'He was a horrible man,' she said.

'Why?' Ray asked. She did not reply. 'Look, I'm investigating his murder, if you have information then I really do need to know. Seriously. What? Did he touch you or hurt you or something?' Ray said, clumsily.

She turned and looked at him, her mouth open. 'Fortunately not, no, since you put it so nicely!' She shook her head and took a deep breath. 'But he was known for it,' she added, pointedly. 'I'm not surprised somebody killed him, he deserved it if anyone ever did. The younger the better. Get it?'

'Yes. Sorry. I deal with a lot of evil people, you know.' He sighed. 'You just get used to it, become a bit blasé about it.'

'Blasé?'

'Yes, like, flippant, off-hand.'

'Oh right.' She considered this. 'Even so, if he had done something to *me* it was not a very nice way of asking about it. Was it?' She sat scowling, clearly still cross.

'Sorry,' Ray said again.

'I think you got it all wrong, anyway,' she continued, vehemently. 'Harris was a dealer. Where you getting your information, hmm? Besides, I told you already, I lived in the docks for like, six, seven weeks. I never saw anyone down there, or saw no boats, no guys smuggling people about.' She shrugged. 'Maybe you should think about what you do know and take it from there.'

Ray considered all this in silence. 'You know, you're very clever,' he said. Ellie gave him an evil look.

'Is that meant to be funny?' she said.

'No,' said Ray. 'It's not.' He stood up from the sofa deep in thought. 'I need to go to the station. I'll be back later.' He stood up and walked to the door. Realising his keys were still on the coffee table, he went back to the sofa and picked them up. Absent-mindedly, he bent down and gave her a kiss on the cheek as he passed. He had taken the three paces to the front door, before he realized what he had just done. He turned back to see Ellie was bright pink. 'Oh, erm…sorry. I wasn't thinking,' Ray said. He paused, then added, 'Did you mind?'

She made a sort of 'Humph' noise. 'Very presumptuous of you,' she said. 'Yes, you heard me. Presumptuous.' Then she put her little nose in the air and turned on the television.

Chapter 42

Frank was sitting at his desk when the knock on his door came. 'Yes,' he stated. Ray walked into his office.

'Guv,' Ray said by way of greeting. 'All right if I shut the door?'

'Surely,' said Frank. 'I thought you might take the day off?' he added, as Ray sat down.

'I just wanted to run through a few things with you. Get them straight in my head. Then I might go home,' said Ray.

Frank nodded. 'I can understand that. What's on your mind?'

'Well,' Ray began, 'I thought there was one, large, organised crime gang working in Tarnside. We had the China White hit the streets and at the same time I saw people getting moved around in the docks. And, obviously, DI Blake was taken hostage. So, I reckoned it had to be one, organised, heavy-duty outfit.'

Frank nodded. 'Yes. Has what happened last night changed your mind?'

'Yes guv. Gary wasn't shot by the people who took Rosie Blake, was he?'

Frank paused. 'I don't know to be honest, Ray. There's always the possibility that they were aiming for Blake.'

'No guv, I don't buy that. They could have killed her anytime.' Ray paused. 'What if there are two gangs. One selling the China White, the other smuggling people.'

Frank thought about it for a moment. 'Go on,' he said.

'Gary had China White in his home. John Harrington was also an active dealer of heroin; I've only just erm…found that out.'

Frank swallowed. He was not sure he wanted to know exactly how Ray had just found that out. 'Right,' he said.

Ray continued, 'We don't really know if Brown and Harrington were involved in the people trafficking at all. Do we?'

Frank sat and thought about this. 'No idea on Harrington. But Brown was clearly dealing that China White. If there are two gangs, why would the people smuggling ring want to swop Blake for Brown, unless he was one of their people?'

'But they didn't swop Blake for Brown. They gave Blake back and Brown was shot dead. And that coincides with what? A certain high profile celebrity in Tarnside, dying of a heroin overdose.'

Frank scratched his head. 'Sorry, but you're losing me a bit here.'

'Gary Brown was dealing a lot of that China White, right? And the media are now all over Tarnside because Courtney Tumbler has died. Suddenly every journalist and private investigator is sniffing around this town, trying to get the inside scoop on who dealt her that stuff. It's attracting a lot of attention. Now, that's not great news if you're quietly trying to smuggle people into the country. You see?'

Frank stood up and took a few thoughtful paces. He turned to Ray. 'We de-briefed Blake this morning. She confirmed the gang asked her about Virtus. She thinks they kidnapped her in error. She said they treated her fairly well, most of the time anyway. That does NOT leave this room, by the way, Ray.'

Ray shook his head. 'No, of course not guv. But do you think I might be right, then? They used Blake to take Brown out because his dealing was attracting the wrong kind of attention to Tarnside? Potentially jeopardising their little trafficking operation?'

Frank scratched his head. 'I'm not sure. I mean, we had him in custody. So from their point of view, surely he was already out of the picture? And how did they know we had nicked Brown, anyway? I've never been clear on that. Seems more likely to me that somebody wanted to silence Brown, permanently, he must have had some information or something. Is Harrington even involved in any of this, why are you so convinced that there's any link at all?'

Suddenly Ray stood up. 'I think I need to go and have a meet with someone. Someone who might hold a lot of answers.'

'Ray,' said Frank, calmly.

'Guv?'

'Ray, you're going to have to put your sources on the books. Officially.'

Ray knew the rules. All informants, in theory at least, needed to be registered and shared with at least one other officer. At Tarnside, Frank stipulated that any Detective Sergeant needed to share his informant with a Detective Inspector, or, alternatively, an even higher ranking officer. Frank also insisted that the relationship, between the informant and the handler, was very closely monitored. Although every member of CID always tried to keep their sources exclusively their own for as long as possible, inevitably, sooner or later, they had to put them on the official records.

'I will guv. Just…just let me have one more chat with him. I can get to the bottom of this.' Ray knew he was asking a lot as a Detective Sergeant, and from an officer who was responsible for the whole of Tarnside CID. He could see Frank wrestling with conflicting emotions. There was a tense silence.

'One more chat, but that's it. And I need to know his name. Informants are dangerous people, Ray. Two officers got shot last night…are you sure that you're not swimming out of your depth?' Frank looked grim. He bent over the desk. 'I nearly lost one officer this week,' he pointed out.

'His name is Ian Grant, guv, he's just a small-time dealer from Brook Hill. Nothing I can't handle.'

'Brook Hill? Whereabouts?' Frank demanded.

'Saffron Court,' Ray replied.

Frank's voice rose a notch or two. 'For fuck's sake Ray, it's a bloody concrete jungle in there! You should know, you worked it closing down that shooting gallery. You can't trust anybody from those blocks!' Frank exhaled, heavily. 'I hope you've got your foot firmly on his throat Ray; because otherwise, you can bet your life, he's certainly got his foot on yours.'

Chapter 43

Frank was genuinely reticent to authorise any further meetings at all between Ray and Ian Grant. He had reminded Ray that they were the police, they had rules to follow, procedures. He had pointed out that this applied to a whole range of different scenarios, emphasising that this included hostage situations. Rules, Frank made clear, that *had* to be followed by those responsible for overseeing these types of operation. Reading between the lines, it was clear to see that Frank was still furious about the whole hostage negotiation last night. It was fairly obvious, to Ray, that Frank felt it had been poorly handled and a missed opportunity to make a pertinent arrest.

An hour later and Ray had told Frank all the information that Ian had supplied him with. Impressed that Ray had managed to glean so much intelligence, Frank then conceded to the meeting on two conditions.

Firstly, Ray was to take the money he had agreed to pay Ian and give it to him. Frank elucidated why it was a useful exercise. Once money had changed hands it gave Ray a little more leverage if he needed it further down the line and it also helped to define the relationship, as employer and employee. 'Psychologically, it's worth every penny, you see?' Frank explained. 'It allows us to take the control back and, what's more, if it ever goes to court for any reason, it's evidence to a jury that he was officially in our employment, as a police informant. For this reason, Ian Grant goes on the books today. Don't worry, you can share him with me on this occasion, nobody else needs to know about him.'

Secondly, Frank wanted them to meet in a public place where he could arrange for a few undercover officers to oversee the meeting, just in case Ian decided to get nasty. He suggested the beachfront, which suited Ray fine. It was clear that Frank was taking no chances and Ray could understand why, particularly given the events of the past few days.

'I'm really am pleased with the way you have handled this, Ray,' Frank summarised. 'You've grown up a lot in the past few weeks. If you had run off and acted like the bloody lone ranger again, we would never have got these results. It's good to see you using our resources, working with the team.' Frank was known to congratulate people; however, to make such a point of it was flattering and relatively rare. Ray felt slightly embarrassed, but it felt good. He thanked his boss and went to leave the room. 'Maybe it's your new *friend*,' Frank teased him as he left the room. 'Something certainly seems to have put a spring in your step.' Frank grinned, as he saw Ray blushing. 'Go on, get out of here. Arrange this meeting and then go home for a bit. I'll need time to get the reccy set-up anyway, so arrange to meet this toe rag tomorrow and let me know the time. Then go home, you soppy sod. Clear?'

'Yes guv,' said Ray. 'Thank you.'

*

Ray walked into the house and found Ellie, now dressed but still watching the television. 'You'll get square eyes watching that thing,' he said, standing behind the sofa.

'Not much else to do, really.' She sounded bored.

'Well, I thought we could go out somewhere, if you fancy it? Anywhere you'd like to go?' Ray offered.

'You back in later, are you?' Ellie enquired, her tone flat.

'Nope,' he replied. 'I'm off now, until tomorrow afternoon. So, what shall we do?' he said.

She looked excited at that news and turned off the television. 'Ooo, well, I don't know,' she replied.

Ellie turned around on the sofa and got up on her knees, not knowing Ray was standing directly behind her. Suddenly, they were face to face. Ray put his arms around her and pulled her close.

'Mmm,' she said 'Nice.' Then she kissed him, gently, slowly, before pulling away and asking him, 'Do you like animals?'

'Well, I sponsor a snow leopard if that counts,' he replied.

'Can we go to a safari park?' she said. She kissed him again, quickly, then put her cheek to his. 'I'll make it worth your while,' she promised and then giggled into his ear.

Two hours later and they were walking through the gates of The Giant Safari Park. The sun was hidden behind a cloud, but Ellie was beaming, telling him how much she had always wanted to visit the place. Like a kid in a candy store, she held his hand and walked around, sometimes breaking away excitedly to look more closely at one of the animals, or read something, before coming back and hooking arms with him again. After they had seen the smaller creatures, they drove through the Big Cat enclosure, then Monkey Zone and then Wolf World and, finally, through The Savannah, where they saw giraffes and elephants and the white rhinos.

'I've never been anywhere like this, you know,' she confided in him as they crawled round the final few stretches of the track. There was a strict no-stopping rule, although people frequently ignored it. Then the park rangers, in white jeeps with black stripes on them, could be seen bouncing over the grass to move them on.

'No, you said before,' Ray laughed. 'I didn't know you were this into animals.'

'Oh, I love animals,' she said, still beaming. 'Don't you?' Looking at Ellie, Ray wondered how he could have fallen for her quite so fast. It had never happened to him before, not like this. Whenever he looked at her, his chest felt like it was being pumped full of something hot.

'Do you want to, erm, be my girlfriend then?' he asked. He caught her by surprise slightly and she turned to look at him from the passenger seat.

'You do know how to pick your moments, don't you?' she teased. She looked at him, her chin jutted up slightly and held his gaze. 'Yes Ray, I will be your girlfriend,' she said seriously, then she giggled again, leant over and kissed him on the cheek. 'Silly,' she said.

'I really like you,' said Ray, then he shut up and faced the front.

Ellie smiled and looked out of the window and there was a brief silence. 'I like you too. But I don't want to rush things. Just so you know that,' she said, softly.

'Good,' he replied, nodding, still looking ahead. 'That's good.'

A second later, Ellie exploded with laughter and punched him on the arm. 'You fucking liar,' she chuckled, making him grin.

*

The drive home took an hour and a half, after which neither of them felt like sitting down very much. Ray suggested they went out for a walk, so they strolled down to the beach, hand in hand.

Ray felt hugely relaxed with Ellie, all the stress and worry that he carried about as a matter of course, all that constant anxiety; it all just seemed to slip away when he was with her. No other girl had ever made him feel like that. In his previous relationships, most of the time he had been made to feel that he was the cause of all the problems; that most of the time, whatever the problem was, it was all his fault. Ellie had never made him feel like that at all.

In contrast, Ellie had never had a serious relationship with anybody. When she looked at Ray, she knew something was special, felt different. But she was in no hurry, either to find out what that feeling may be, or to get deeply involved with anybody at all. She had already decided he would have to be patient and he seemed fine with that, which was just as well as far as she was concerned. Ellie had fought off a few advances in the past, once with a closed fist. Now, relaxed and happy, she gazed over the ocean, where the sun was setting in a hue of red, the sky streaked with yellow and pink. She smiled and thought how beautiful it looked.

'So,' Ray said, 'how about we go and grab something to eat?'

'What, like, in a restaurant?' Ellie did not sound very sure about that idea.

'Well, yeah,' said Ray. 'Curry?'

'Oh yes,' she smiled. 'Oh, I like curry!'

Chapter 44

Above the pebbled beach, three benches were nestled into the grassy slope. Every year, in March, all three of them were repainted a dark green by the council. The steep shoreline of the beach had large red signs spaced along it, warning of the rip tides and deep water. Although swimming was not forbidden, the steep incline into the depths, coupled with the ferocious currents, meant that the beach was only popular with dog walkers and the local fishermen, the latter gathering in large numbers when the bass ran through in the warmer months.

Despite the knowledge that two plain clothes officers were close by, watching the proceedings from an unmarked vehicle, Ray felt nervous as he approached the benches. He had never felt on edge before when meeting up with Ian Grant. He had begun to think of him as confidant, almost as a friend. His chat with Frank had certainly put that into perspective. Ian Grant was a dangerous animal.

Ian was seated, on the far left of the bench furthest away from Ray as he approached, walking down the pebbled beach. Seeing him coming, Ian caught his eye and nodded. He was wearing a grey tracksuit and a pair of white trainers. The sleeves were rolled up and Ian sat hunched over, leaning on his legs. 'Easy bruv,' he said, black eyes squinting in the sunlight.

'All right Ian,' said Ray, sitting down. They sat for a moment in silence.

'You got something for me, then?' Ian prompted him.

'Yeah, I have,' Ray replied. 'I've got your money in my pocket.'

'Cheers bruv, nice one,' Ian replied. There was a short silence, broken only by a seagull on the beach.

Then Ray spoke up. 'We've got a bit of a problem, though, you and me,' he stated, calmly.

Ian looked at him slyly. 'Why, what's up geez?' he asked.

'I've come into some new information. John Harrington, or Harris, he was dealing in heroin, black tar to be specific.' Ray let the words hang in the air, waiting for Ian to break the silence.

'Oh yeah?' Ian said. 'Wouldn't surprise me, bruv. What's the problem? He's dead now, init?'

'Yes,' said Ray, 'he's dead all right. But it was nothing to do with people trafficking.' Ray turned to look at Ian. 'Was it, Ian?'

Ian shifted slightly on the bench. He pulled a face and shrugged a shoulder. 'If you say so, I ain't gonna argue wiv ya.' He returned his stare to the ocean in front of them.

'Then there's Gary Brown.' Ray watched Ian closely. Nothing flickered on his face, nothing at all.

'You picked him up, didn't you? I done my bit, bruv.'

Ray started to push a bit harder. 'Oh yeah, we picked him up all right. And guess what we found at his house, Ian.'

Ian shrugged. 'Bit of weed or summin'?'

'Twenty grand's worth of pure heroin.' Ian did not even flinch. Ray continued, 'The same stuff that killed Courtney Tumbler, Ian. Now, there's a lot of people out there that loved Courtney Tumbler and a lot of them, have a lot of money. Now, here's what I think. I wasn't the only person you told about Gary Brown. Somebody else offered you a lot of money to tell them where Brown could be found. But by then, you'd already shopped him to me for five hundred quid. When someone offered you a lot more, you devised a plan to get him out into the open. Brown and Harrington are nothing to do with any people smuggling, they just deal drugs. But you, you're involved with the other gang, aren't you? Aren't you, Ian?'

Ian did not say anything. 'Why do you think Harrington was dealing then, eh?' Ian looked at him coldly and Ray felt threatened for the first time. 'Who told you that, then?' said Ian, quietly.

'I know he was, Ian. A witness came forward. After Harris was already dead.'

Ian turned away and looked back out to sea. He shrugged. 'Probably just some junkie tart,' he said. 'That won't stand up.'

'No, she's not some junkie tart,' said Ray, his temper flaring slightly.

Ian looked at him out of the corner of his eyes again. 'Oh yeah? Why, you fucking her? What, tell you she was a virgin, did she?'

Ian looked back at the sea and laughed, scornfully. 'Why do you think she was scoring off Harris, then, eh?'

'For a friend,' Ray replied, honestly.

Ian sat there, measuring Ray's response and then he looked back out to sea and nodded his head a few times. 'Ha,' he said. 'You go tell that to a jury.'

'How's the family, Ian?'

Once again, Ian did not bat an eyelid. Ray began to realize what he was up against. 'Yeah, all right mate.' Ian turned to look at Ray. 'How's yours?'

'I don't have one, Ian. But you've got a kid now, haven't you? You thought about her future? Is it Saffron Court for her? That's what you want, is it?'

Ian started to lose his temper and Ray could see he had finally managed to rattle him, which had been his intention. 'What the fuck is it to you? Eh?' Ray stared at Ian, confrontationally. This had the desired effect. 'You want to watch your mouth, init. Talk about my family?' Ian jabbed a finger towards his face. 'I'll slit your throat while you sleep, bruv. Fucking believe it.'

Ian looked at him, tight lipped, fuming. He was a formidable character when he was angry. They faced each other.

'Listen to me,' said Ray, roughly. 'Brown was shot dead last night. People want answers. The way things look at the moment, you're an accessory to murder. That's life, Ian. I'm not threatening your family, for fuck's sake. I'm not some sick fuck. I'm trying to make you think about them for the right reasons. If you don't start talking, I can't help you. You understand? It's too big. It's out of my hands already. If you level with me, I can still get you out of this, or at least plead your case at court, but you're running out of time and it's not going to just go away.' Ray took a breath. 'I know there are two gangs, Ian. I actually came here to try and help you.'

Ian was looking away, swiftly calming down. In a minute, the moment would be gone. Before Ray could say anything further, Ian spoke up. 'When I said to you I was thinking about becoming a copper, right, that was true. I was. But I can't do that. I'm not like you. I'm involved, init? I got people leaning on me for this and that, you get me?'

'Every undercover officer is always involved Ian, how the hell do you think we ever nick anybody? There's a reason our prisons are overflowing. And you should see the technology we have now, the forensics, everything. Nobody can get away with it anymore. Please. Think about it. Make the right choice. Tomorrow, it really might be too late.'

Ian scratched his eyebrow. He looked anxious now. 'They're coming for me, init?' Ray did not reply. 'I was trying to help you, bruv.'

Ray gave him a look that suggested he found that hard to believe. 'Look,' Ray told him, 'I haven't got it all worked yet. Why don't you *really* help me, yeah? Then I can explain how you were of assistance. Before that window, closes.' Ian said nothing. 'Last chance Ian and it's out of my hands. You can take the five hundred quid, but we're done and I can't protect you.' Ray shrugged. 'I really can't, mate,' he said, honestly.

Ian put a hand to his forehead. 'You know, I like you Ray,' Ian said. Ray sat in silence. 'Most coppers, they're not like you bruv.'

'No. I know,' said Ray. Suddenly he realized that he had finally got through to Ian, somehow. 'Most people in Saffron Court, Ian; they're not like you, either.'

'No,' Ian replied. 'I know.' They looked at each other for a second. Worlds apart.

'It's not too late for you,' Ray said.

Ian's head went back like he had just been pushed. He snorted. 'You don't know, bruv. You don't live where I live.'

'You don't have to live there. You don't,' Ray insisted. 'You're very bright.'

Ian laughed suddenly. 'Well look, if you already know that there's two gangs having a turf war, I don't really know what more I can tell ya!'

Chapter 45

It hit Ray like a thunderbolt. *A turf war.* This was all about the control of the turf. Drugs. Heroin. This was about controlling the supply of the heroin.

'So, whose side are you on?' Ray asked him.

Ian looked at him and smiled. 'Me? I'm on everybody's side, bruv. That's how I keep walking around.'

'Harrington just dealt tar. I don't understand how Gary Brown fits into all of this, Ian. Help me out here.'

Ian tutted and rolled his eyes. 'Blimey, it's a wonder you lot lock anyone up. Brown and Harris, right,' he said, slowly. Ray nodded. 'They were the main dealers of H, okay? Harris dealt Grove Square and Brown dealt up Brook Hill. What's funny right, is Brown dealt brown.' Ian laughed for a moment.

'So who took out Harris? Did he owe money?'

'Nah, new firm. Moved down from London. Dealing all this new China White. See?'

Ray still looked confused. 'But, why didn't they just sell it to him to deal instead, why kill him?'

'Well, just sending a message, like, you know. Harris was hated by a lot of people anyways, so I guess he was just an easy target bruv.' Ian shrugged. 'They was moving in. New firm, new people; that's just how it is.'

'So people really were looking for Gary Brown?' Ray asked

'Yeah, I wasn't, like, totally bullshitting you. Gary, he thought he was, like, a proper gangsta and he was *nothing*, bruv. Fucking joker.'

Ray nodded. 'Yeah, I get it.' He saw Ian nodding as well. 'So,' Ray continued, 'People leant on you to get Brown nicked, right?'

'Yeah,' said Ian. 'I was getting paid by you and by them. Clever, init?'

Suddenly it dawned on Ray. 'So the heroin we found in Gary's house had been planted. Was that you?'

'Oh, that. Well. What's the difference? He was dealing the stuff anyway, brown, white, whatever. He had it coming, bruv. It was about time someone did something anyway. Dealing to kids and that, the pair of them.'

Ray took this in for a moment. 'So, once he'd been set-up, why bother taking him out? He was going down anyway, for a long, long time.'

'Yeah,' said Ian. 'Well, I kinda thought that was the plan myself, to be honest wiv ya.'

'That was your idea, wasn't it?' Ray said. 'Because you were talking to me?'

Ian shrugged. 'Couldn't say, bruv. But better off inside than dead, init? I had nothing to do with him getting shot. In fact, that's news to me. How the fuck did that happen?'

'The people you know had abducted one of our officers, they were holding her prisoner.'

'Oh yeah, but she weren't hurt or nothing. That was just to keep you lot busy. No harm.'

'No harm?' Ray said, incredulous. 'They asked to exchange her for Brown and she nearly got killed, two officers were shot and Brown is dead.'

Ian blanched slightly. 'Oh, right.' He sat and thought about it. 'Quite clever, though. I mean, like, it makes the whole immigrant thing seem real, right, so keeps you busy chasing around in the dark: chasing the wrong crime, let alone any idea what people it is.'

Then Ian smiled. 'Ah, nah, I see it. It's that Courtney bird. You know, that celebrity? They needed a fall guy. And I bet you thought the geezer what dealt the China to that Courtney bird was dead as well, init?'

Ray nodded, slowly. 'Yes, we did. Actually, I was thinking earlier that Gary Brown and the death of Courtney Tumbler and the China White we found in his flat must all be connected.'

Ian gave him a look. 'That's it. But someone was a few steps ahead of you. And dead men don't talk.'

Ray sat in silence for a moment, digesting all this information. Then he turned to Ian again. 'I suppose that little sideshow at the docks, that was for my benefit as well, was it?'

Ian chuckled. 'Yeah. Should have seen the look on your face, bruv.' He fished into his pocket and pulled out his phone. 'Here, this is a good one.' He flicked through some of the photos and held one up of Ray, standing by the wire fence in the pouring rain, looking terrified. 'Gotta laugh, int'cha?'

Ray looked at the photo of himself and then looked at Ian. 'So,' Ray said slowly, 'there's no people smuggling going on at all.'

'Nah. I thought you said you knew there was two gangs, anyway?' Ian asked, suddenly suspicious.

'I was close, but I had it slightly wrong.' Ray reflected on Ian's situation. 'So they've been forcing you to feed me all this bullshit? How did they know that you knew me in the first place, anyway?'

Ian pulled a face and looked out to sea. He took a moment to reply. 'You should never have come and found me outside the manor. You was seen. Eyes is always watching. And I was seen, getting in your motor. You brought a lot of this on yourself, bruv. And on my head and all.' Ian exhaled heavily. He looked miserable.

The two of them sat together for a few minutes. A flock of seagulls descended on the beach, fighting over something one of the birds had spotted.

Ray spoke up. 'Why did you say that, about the woman who informed on Harris? About her saying she was a virgin?'

Ian looked over to Ray for a second. 'You are banging her, aren't you? Fucking hell, I hope you're joking, bruv. Serious!'

'No. I'm not sleeping with her. But I did give her a place to stay, to get herself sorted out. She's only young, younger than you,' Ray told him.

Dumbfounded, Ian sat staring at Ray for about five seconds. Then he just asked, 'Why?'

'I don't know. I felt sorry for her,' Ray replied. 'She's a nice girl.'

Ian pulled his ear for a minute, staring out to sea. Then he scratched his forehead and shuffled in his seat. After that, he started shaking his head. He sat for a moment in thought, before remembering Ray's question. 'Oh, no reason I said it, bruv. I don't know her, no idea who she is.' Ian shrugged. 'That's what all the girls say, init.' He looked away, to his left, then turned and looked straight at him. 'Just be careful, yeah? No offence, like, but you're not the most streetwise copper I ever had a chat with, know what I mean?'

Ray nodded. They sat in silence for a few moments. Ray glanced at Ian and saw he looked a bit upset, almost looked like he was going to cry for some reason, which Ray could not really understand.

'You know,' Ray said, 'if you join the police force, you get sent away for twelve weeks training. Three months minimum. Then you often get posted outside of your home town.'

Ian looked at Ray. 'Nah, I din't know that. That right, is it?'

'Yeah,' said Ray. 'I'm not from round here, for example.'

'Sounds all right, though. Fresh start,' said Ian, squinting hard into the distance.

Ray paused. 'So, you gonna help me nail Parkes and finish this?' he asked.

Ian looked genuinely surprised. 'Parkes? How do you know about Parkes?'

'I told you Ian, we're all over it.'

'This your little birdie talking again, is it?' Ian asked.

'No,' Ray lied. 'Another source. If you deal drugs and then lots of people suddenly start to die, or end up in hospital, people talk. You must know that we went to talk to Parkes and he did a runner?'

Ian nodded. 'Yeah, I know.'

'Well…innocent people don't run away from the police. He kind of fucked himself there.'

'Well…I can't tell you where he is, they'll know it was me that grassed. You'll have to find him yourself…try your *other source*,' Ian replied, sarcastically.

'Hmm…well, as I say Ian, you're an accessory to murder at the moment. So, it seems to me, you're between a rock and a hard place.'

Chapter 46

Ian Grant was bothered that Ray had taken into his home some random, homeless girl who was scoring tar. The sort of junkie bitch he used to kick out the abandoned flats on the estate, if he ever found them hiding in there. 'Don't want none of that round my gaff,' he used to tell his girlfriend. Something about Ray's random act of kindness had caught him out, thrown all his emotions off-balance. Walking back to his car with the money that Ray had promised him, Ian did not know quite how to feel about what Ray had done. He felt slightly mixed up inside. Suddenly, Ian was confronting a range of issues that he had never even questioned how he should feel about.

Ian had, wrongly, supposed that most homeless people were junkies and therefore he had never felt any pity for any of them. Junkie just meant scum to Ian. Trash. No-one forced them to stick a needle in their arm. Now, already considering the life he wanted to give his baby daughter, he was questioning some of his own attitudes as well. Conflicting emotions rattled around in his head, jarring constantly. To his frustration, he could not marry them together.

Grudgingly, Ian was forced to admit to himself that Ray's act of kindness had now affected his own way of thinking. Ian reflected that, if Ray had said she was a nice girl, then she probably was. And that meant that not *all* homeless people were simply vermin. A few years ago Ian had personally instigated, quite deliberately, the policy of ousting vermin from the disused flats on the estate. 'Taking out the trash', he had joked with his mates at the time. Now driving home, Ian shook his head, wrapped deeply in his own thoughts.

Arriving back at Saffron Court, Ian parked his car and looked up at the tower block in front of him that he called home. He saw a few of the local kids running down the steps, laughing and shouting, then he heard a far older voice from further up, calling out. It was an elderly woman, she sounded frightened. Ian jumped out of his car and walked swiftly over to the staircase, arriving just in time to catch one of the kids by the scruff of the neck as he tried to run past him. 'What's your game then, eh?' he demanded, almost lifting the kid off his feet. The kid opened his mouth, then took one look at Ian and shut it again. 'I see you here again, upsetting the old folk, I'll chuck you off that fucking balcony.' Ian held him, angry. The kid only looked about nine or ten. Ian pushed his grubby little face up to the sky. 'You see it?' he said, pointing at the railings a few floors up. 'Now, fuck off,' he said. The kid scarpered, running after his friends who were already rapidly diminishing blots on the horizon. When the youngster was out of earshot, Ian called up, 'It's all right Mrs. Johnson. Just kids.'

He trudged up the concrete steps and into his flat on the first floor. His girlfriend was on the sofa and their daughter lay in her arms, both of them fast asleep. The baby girl was still tiny and had kept both Ian and his partner up for most of the night. Ian fetched himself a beer out of the fridge and cracked it open, before sitting down on an armchair, still deep in thought.

***

Ray sat on the bench for a long time after Ian had gone on his way, different thoughts also rattling around in his mind. He reflected that it was true, he was not very streetwise, especially when he compared himself to Ian Grant. Something about the way Ian had spoken about Ellie, even if he did not know her personally, had taken the rose-tinted glasses off his face. Ray looked at the facts more coldly, more objectively. He barely knew the girl and he had no reason to trust her. She might be taking him for a complete fool. That had happened to him once before, after all. Last night, she had certainly not been very forward, just a kiss and a cuddle on the sofa. Maybe she was just using him for free meal and a bed. Perhaps she was still using altogether.

When Ray finally opened his front door it was early evening. Ellie was sitting on the sofa, watching the television. She turned and smiled at him. 'Hello,' she said. Ray nodded and went into the kitchen. 'You all right?' she said.

'Yeah, fine,' he said, brusquely.

She frowned a bit, then shrugged. 'Okay,' she said and turned back to the television. He was quite moody, she reflected.

Ray came and sat down on the sofa. 'You don't know an Ian Grant, do you?' he asked. She shook her head.

'Nope,' she said. 'Why do you ask?'

'Oh, no reason. Just something he said to me,' Ray replied. 'For a minute, I thought maybe he knew you, but he said he didn't, anyway. Just checking.'

'Nope, I don't know anyone called Ian. To be honest, I don't know many people round here at all. Not been here that long, really,' she said. Ray nodded but sat in silence. 'You want to know a bit more about me, huh?' she said.

Ray nodded. 'Yeah, maybe a bit,' he said.

She nodded and took a deep breath. 'Okay, well, I finished college, like, did my A levels. Didn't do that great, though.' She paused and looked away. Then she started again.

'Things were fine until my Dad died. When I was thirteen, he died in a car accident. My Mum started drinking a lot, well...that's when I really noticed it anyway. She got together with another guy pretty quickly. They both drank a lot.'

Ellie paused. 'He used to knock me about a bit, but I never told anyone. One day, my Mum came home and saw him hitting me and then he left, but her drinking got worse. By the time I started college at sixteen, I was spending a lot of time at friends' houses and stuff. Then, when that finished, I got a bar job and had a room in a shared house. But I bust my ankle and I couldn't work for a while and...I met different people. Spent some time with them...they weren't paying rent, just squatting this big house, which was cool at first. But then we got kicked out and I got a bit stuck.' She took a deep breath. 'Things were bad for a few months, but then I met you.' She smiled at him, but her blue eyes looked sad.

'That sounds pretty tough,' Ray replied. Ellie shrugged. There was a brief pause. 'Is your Mum still around then?' Ray asked her. 'She's probably worried about you.'

'Oh, I been ringing her a bit,' Ellie answered. 'I was, erm...going to mention that to you.'

'It's fine,' Ray replied. He closed his eyes and sat back. 'Ring her whenever you like.' She came over to where he was sitting on the sofa and cuddled up to him, putting her head under his chin.

'Thank you,' she said. He could feel her breathing, heavily. 'She was pleased I was okay,' Ellie said quietly. Then Ray realized she was crying again. He cuddled her back, properly.

'Good,' he said. He felt her calming down as he stroked her hair, gently. 'You've had a rough few years, but things will get better now,' he promised her. 'You'll meet someone and life will get better.'

She pulled away and looked at him. 'But I've met you,' she said. Ray smiled at her, but he already felt like she was a million miles away.

'Yeah,' he said. 'But you should be with someone your own age.'

Her mouth dropped open and Ray knew that look by now. 'Don't judge me!' she said, hotly. 'I can choose my own boyfriends. I hardly think some spotty, nineteen year old bloke is going to understand me, do you? All they think about is getting their end away!'

Ray struggled with his own emotions. 'I…I don't know,' he said. 'I'm just a lonely man, I'm really not your problem. I don't want to take advantage of…of your situation.' He looked at her, helplessly. 'It's difficult for me,' he said, weakly.

She sat up and quickly sat astride him, sticking her knees into the sofa cushions behind him, pinning him down and putting her arms around his neck.

The mobile phone on the sofa arm bleeped a couple of times, signalling a text message. Ray pulled away from her and picked it up. The message that had flashed up on his phone was from Ian Grant. It read *"113 Temple Avenue. Top floor. Gone by 2nite"*.

Chapter 47

Detective Superintendent Paul Harding just had that look.

Dangerous. True gangster. A man that would grab you by the neck and ram your head through iron railings without a second's hesitation. His blonde hair had recently been cropped very short again, but he had not shaved for a few days and his pale, blue eyes looked even more closed than usual. Wearing an ankle length, black leather coat he stood, lean and mean at 6'2", chewing his cheek like an angry wasp.

Directly behind him stood Ray and Jason, one on each shoulder, flanking him. Further back stood eight uniformed officers, dressed in full riot gear, including boots, knee pads, shin guards, thigh pads, stab proof vests and blue, police helmets. Two of the uniformed officers were trained as part of the Force Support Group, or FSG, and they held a Double-Rammit between them. They faced the steel door in front of them.

The Double-Rammit is a metre long battering ram that weighs twenty-four kilograms and impacts with ferocious power. Whereas the one man, Single-Rammit impacts with six thousand, three hundred kilograms of kinetic force, the Double-Rammit - seven kilograms heavier and roughly a third longer - will impact with almost three times that energy when wielded by skilled operators. If that failed to stove the door in, there were other options. Paul had instructed the FSG team to bring, what he called, 'the whole box of tricks'. This includes items such as the hydraulic 'Spreader', a pneumatic tool known as the 'Blower' (which also uses air pressure), bolt croppers, a steel spreading tool known as the Galena, a selection of sledgehammers and a Eurolock snapper and puller tool, used to break europrofile locks and enable easy entry. In short, Paul Harding was going in.

The men stared through their face visors at the Detective Superintendent. In addition to the protective clothing all the men were wearing, two of the Constables also held full body-length riot shields.

Paul turned to Ray. 'This is the place. You're sure?'

'Yes,' he replied. 'This is the place. Top floor.'

The building was situated down a quiet back street in the town centre. It was non-descript, square and brick, home to a garage workshop on the ground floor. As it was now eight o'clock at night the garage was closed, a steel shutter rolled down and firmly locked in place with two, heavy-duty, external padlocks, both running through galvanised iron brackets cemented into the wall on both sides. Also on the front, to the left side of the workshop and built into the ground floor block, was a small, glass fronted office that served as a reception area. A modest, private forecourt held a few parked cars, presumably on-site for repairs or servicing of some kind.

The left of the building was directly adjacent to a brick wall, roughly twelve feet high, with barely three inches between the two. The high brick wall continued around the back of the block, surrounding a small car-park to the rear which had a singular, narrow entrance on the right. An external, metal, staircase ran down the back of the three-storey building and served as a fire escape, presumably installed as part of mandatory fire regulations to enable the upper floor to be legally rented out to commercial tenants.

Around the right side, a heavy-duty, flat steel door with no handle was set about six inches into the brick wall, near to the rear of the block. The door was a faded blue, unmarked and it opened out directly onto the small, narrow and unlit back lane. This lane also served as a back entrance to a row of terraced houses; a selection of broken fences, boards and panels lining the track. Consisting solely of compacted gravel and mud, the track was bumpy, dotted with parked vehicles and dustbins.

Paul, Ray, Jason and four officers, two with the Double-Rammit, were congregated in the shadows by the metal door. Paul lifted a radio to his mouth and spoke into it, softly. 'Stand by all units. Tango tangos, in position at the rear?'

'Standing by,' came the clear response.

'Cover position, I repeat, I want cover first and foremost while we breach. Do not mount the staircase and proceed to enter until I give the order. I want those two shields covering that staircase.

Remember, shields up first, the other two follow. Is that understood?' Paul instructed the officers, who now stood tensely at the foot of the fire escape staircase.

'Understood, standing by, over.'

Paul stood facing the doorway. He lifted both arms and motioned to Ray and Jason to stand to each side, before he stepped aside himself and waved forward the uniformed officers holding the battering ram.

Paul turned. He looked briefly into the face of all six men, scanning them. 'Ready?' he said. 'Uniform in first, then we follow. Okay! Hit it!'

Immediately, the two Constables swung back the battering ram and smashed it into the metal door with all the force they could muster. The sound was tremendous - but nothing gave.

'Again!' shouted Paul.

The officers took even paces back. It was rare for the door not to go first time, often completely from its hinges. Expertly trained, the men took a set stance once more, looked at one another, nodded, and then swung the giant metal ram back, far and high. Propelling their momentum forward together, they let out grunts of exertion as it smashed into the steel door. They caught the door far more accurately this time, precisely on top of the only visible keyhole, centre left. The full pressure of the blow caused something to audibly crack, possibly some sort of long bolt or steel girder was loosened. Paul held his fists up, clenched. A gesture of triumph.

'One more time!' he shouted, gleefully.

Jason glanced at Ray, his expression implying he thought Paul was a bit of a nutcase. Ray nodded, then suddenly grinned. It was so obvious that Paul was clearly right in his element. Ray surmised that the lack of action that Paul's role now entailed, as Detective Superintendent, was probably something to do with it. The tedium of months of paperwork was now being unleashed, he looked like a man ready to jump into a cage fight. No wonder, Ray reflected, he had such a formidable reputation. It was clearly well-earned.

The ram smashed into the door for the third time and with a crunching groan it gave in; the whole process had taken less than twenty seconds. It tottered for a moment and Paul helped it on its way with the flat of his right foot, clad in an ankle-high, steel-capped boot. The steel door crashed inwards, crumpled. Paul turned to the uniformed officers, eyes suddenly wide open, lending him a wild and terrifying appearance. Simultaneously clicking the radio, he raised a fist above his head like a man starting a race, then brought it down as he bellowed into the mouthpiece, 'ALL UNITS! GO GO GO!'

Chapter 48

A flight of bare concrete steps lay straight ahead of them. The two police Constables, who had stood aside to enable the FSG team to gain access, now sprinted forward. The stairway was dark, narrow and steep. The other two officers then dropped the Double-Rammit rather clumsily, to the right-hand side of the doorway, before following their colleagues into the building. Paul stood behind them, snorting, an angry animal on an invisible leash.

'GO!' he thundered. Pushing the leading figure forward roughly from behind, Paul inadvertently caused the man to lose his balance and trip over the crumpled, steel door which now lay in the bottom stairwell. Unable to contain himself any longer, Paul leapt over him and started charging up the flight of seventeen, concrete steps, yelling and shouting something that sounded vaguely like 'Police', with a few choice curses thrown in for good measure. As the other two leading officers reached the door at the foot of the stairs, a sickening sound rang out. A deafening BANG. The leading officer flew back into his partner behind him, the force knocking them both down the stairwell and on top of Paul, who was halfway up.

'FUCK!' shouted Paul, bringing the radio to his mouth. 'TANGO TANGO, STAND DOWN, STAND DOWN. SUSPECTS ARMED, I REPEAT, SHOTS FIRED, SHOTS FIRED!'

The other two Constables remained static at the foot of the stairs, frozen to the spot, whilst Ray craned his head round the frame of the door, unsure of what to do either. As he watched, he saw Paul halfway up the steps, labouring under the weight of a dead man whose stomach had been ripped open by the blast. Blood and entrails spilled onto the concrete. Above him, a wooden door swung slowly, a round hole in it, over a foot across. A shotgun had blazed through it at the precise moment the officer had reached the top of the steps. The following officer, behind him, had been blown back down the stairway with such force he had almost been knocked out cold. One arm now clutched at the wooden handrail, as he tried to stand near to the foot of the steps.

Ray could only watch as a figure appeared at the top of the stairway, holding a sawn off shotgun in two hands. Pointing it down the steps at Paul, he caught sight of the two FSG officers and Ray's head in the doorway. Changing his mind, the man raised the barrel and fired. Ray ducked back as a second, ear-splitting blast rang out down the concrete stairwell. The officer next to him crumpled, his face a distorted mass of bright, bright red, punctures in his neck still pumping blood, splattering the walls and steps as he collapsed with a stuttering, jerking movement. Blood streamed from his body and pooled rapidly over the blue, steel door. Paul tumbled past Ray out of the doorway, slipping in the fresh blood and almost falling, scrambling round the door frame and out of the line of fire. Ray reached inside with an arm and grabbed the dazed Constable, desperately trying to pull him to safety. Seeing what he was doing, the remaining uniform ducked around him, seized the man's stab vest with two hands and, between them, they managed to drag the officer out into the night.

'I'm reloading,' said a calm voice. 'Then I'm going to come downstairs. Then I'm going to kill the rest of you.'

At the rear of the building the other four uniformed officers had evidently used their initiative. The police van they had arrived in was now parked sideways across the narrow car-park entrance, completely blocking access. The wall was too high for anybody to climb over without a ladder, so it was obvious that their strategy had been one of containment. They were gathered beside the van, their backs to the wall, awaiting instructions.

Now down to five men, including Paul, and with one too concussed to be of any use, the group that had come under fire looked to their boss for leadership. Standing alongside him, Ray watched him run a hand over his face. He looked unsure of what action to take. Ray spoke quietly to him, 'I can try and talk him down, stall him, if you can bring in a firearms unit?'

'This isn't bloody London, Raymond! We don't have SCO19 cruising around Tarnside, waiting for the next incident to respond to. It can be arranged to bring in a Firearms Unit, through SOCA, but that takes preparation, time.' Ray saw that Paul was close to losing control of his emotions completely. 'We're not geared for this shit,' Paul hissed at him, looking slightly desperate. He reached for the radio and started to call in an ambulance and report the situation to Dispatch, requesting back-up.

Jason grabbed Ray's arm. Staring behind them, he addressed them both. 'What the fuck?' he said.

Two Jankel, Guardian MRV units had just screeched round the corner at the top of the road and were now hurtling towards them, bouncing down the lane. As they all watched, gobsmacked, a man in a flak jacket with ARMED POLICE written on it, leant out of the vehicle and shouted down the lane, 'Get that fucking van moved! Do it, NOW!'

The four uniformed officers leapt into action, one of them sprinting to the van door and unlocking it, the others running over to join Paul and their group. Suddenly, everything started to move very fast.

One of the MRV vehicles swung into the car-park area behind the building, the other pulled up literally feet from the broken door where they were gathered. Four officers burst from the back of the vehicle, fully kitted up with Kevlar body armour, ceramic helmets, and assault vests loaded with stun grenades and tear gas. In addition, all the men wore gas masks of some kind. Ray recognised the weaponry they held, one with a Benelli M3 Super 90 shotgun, two holding MP5 sub machine guns and the other clutching an HK G3k assault rifle.

The SFO unit barely glanced at them, simply moved into position and did what they were trained to do. The two holding MP5 machine guns took positions at the foot of the staircase, one on each side. The man with the Benelli took a position alongside the man on the right. The other man holding the assault rifle stood a few feet away from the doorway, to the left and held a radio. He spoke into it, calmly. 'Papa Papa calling two six five. Tear gas?' he said. The radio report came back through.

'Papa Zulu two six five receiving, no windows visible at the rear, one external fire exit staircase, door is closed. Suggest we cover position, over.'

The armed officer in front of Paul saw the blood flowing through the doorway for the first time. 'Negative two six five, shots fired, we have a man down, repeat a man down. Look to take aggressive stance. Can you confirm?'

'Papa Zulu two six five, message received, we are currently proceeding to the external staircase. Happy to take an aggressive stance. Currently standing by to storm position. Please confirm. Over.'

The man holding the assault rifle turned to Paul and smiled, briefly. 'What are you doing here, soldier?'

Ray saw Paul smile back and realized the two men obviously knew one another. 'What the fuck are you lot doing here, more like?' Paul enquired.

'Saving your arse again, by the looks of it. We've been tracking this mob for months.' He winked at Paul. 'I heard you got to the party a little early. We'll talk later.' The man spoke into his radio. 'This is Papa Papa. Confirm two six five, prepare to engage. Repeat. Prepare to engage. Over.'

Chapter 49

The SFO unit worked so fast that the whole event was over in minutes. Firstly, they threw a disproportionate amount of tear gas up the stairwell, a minute later this was followed by several stun grenades. Confirming on the radio that the rear entrance was being simultaneously assaulted, the four officers raced up the steps, brandishing their various weapons and shouting that they were the armed police.

Everybody at ground level knew that in a situation like this, where two police officers had just been killed, the SFO unit would be keen to shoot to kill and ask questions later. The only way the man, or men, upstairs could avoid being shot dead would be to lie face down, on the floor, outstretched, so when the armed officers entered the room they had no excuse to pull the trigger.

Within seconds, Ray heard a Benelli shotgun at the rear, blasting through the hinges of the fire door using breaching rounds, then an MP5 on the stairwell above him rattling out a few shots, before more shouting came from the back. 'Armed Police, get down, down on the floor, do it, do it NOW!'

Within just a few minutes, two men were being led out of the building coughing and choking, their eyes bright red and streaming. Both men appeared Oriental - neither of them was Tony Parkes.

Then a third man was brought out of the building in handcuffs. None other than Ian Grant. He did not so much as glance at Ray as he was placed into the van alongside the other two men.

Ray stepped forward and spoke up loudly, silently praying that the Detective Superintendent, or another officer from SOCA, would not question him. 'I want the prisoners split up immediately,' Ray commanded. 'You two,' he pointed at Ian and a face he did not recognise. 'Out.' The two men got out of the van. Ray turned to find Jason, who fortunately was standing right behind him. 'Take this one, put him in a cell on his own, clear?' he said, pointing at Ian. 'I'll take this other piece of filth myself.'

Jason nodded. He had no idea who Ian Grant was and simply man-handled him as he would any prisoner. 'Let's go, sunshine,' he said.

'Isolation,' Ray called after them. He held his breath as Jason placed Ian into a squad car, got in the back with him and a uniform drove them away. At that moment, Paul came striding over to him, looking fairly annoyed.

Ray turned and looked at him, his back to the prisoner behind him. 'I am isolating the prisoners, Sir.' Paul stopped a moment as Ray's expression caught his eye. Ray never called him, 'Sir'.

There was a brief pause. 'Very good, Detective Sergeant. I dare say that SOCA will want to have a word with them all in any case. Carry on.'

Ray turned back around. 'Where's my man, Parkes?' he said across the car-park, loudly, to no-one in particular. Turning and glancing at the man he had taken from the back of the police van, Ray saw the prisoner's face change completely. His mouth puckered like an angry monkey and fury glittered in his eyes. 'Parkes is dead,' said the man in handcuffs. 'How you know Parkes?' he demanded. Ray saw the bait had been taken.

'Dead? Shot?' Ray enquired of him.

'Upstairs,' the man confirmed. Ray pretended that he was upset about this news for a second or two, but he was careful not to overdo it. Simply looked at the ground and shook his head a few times. Then he grabbed the prisoner roughly.

'Time to go,' Ray told him.

***

'Triads?' Frank exclaimed. 'In Tarnside?'

'Apparently so, Frank,' Paul replied. 'Some sort of Chinese gang, anyway. Based in London. In Chinatown, obviously.'

The two men were sitting outside in the garden of The Royal Oak, a popular haunt for the local force. Situated within walking distance of the station, the pub served good food and had a large garden.

'I can't believe what we've had to deal with recently,' Frank stated, shaking his head. 'It won't be long before we're all armed, I dare say. I'll be glad to be out of it by then, I can tell you.'

'Hmm, I used to think that. What happened last night might have changed my mind though,' Paul admitted.

'You're lucky you weren't killed, Paul.'

'Yeah. Probably. Still, five kilos of heroin is a good result,' he said, taking a slurp on his pint.

'I dare say all the trouble in Burma has something to do with it. And Laos, the whole place is a tinderbox. I heard rumours a few years back that the Laos government were producing heroin in laboratories, that the production was state-funded. I thought it was laughable. Nowadays, I'm not so sure.'

Paul pulled a face. 'The Golden Triangle? Always been a major producer of heroin. A lot of it was being imported from there a few decades ago.'

'Yes,' Frank said, nodding his agreement. 'It mostly got stamped out, though. Back when the firearms squad were a little less, erm, refined in their approach. Especially in London.'

Paul laughed loudly. 'The firearms squad?' he said. 'Fucking cowboys, the lot of them, especially a few decades back. Not like that now, though.'

Frank took a swig of his drink. 'Hmm…maybe not. I guess the racism, absolutely endemic within the force when I joined, has now been stamped out for the most part. But how much else has actually changed? I don't know really. I can tell you one thing though, when I was walking the beat people had a lot more respect for the law. Not because they were less bent Paul, just because they feared us.'

Paul nodded his agreement. 'When I was in the armed forces, it was the same. Respect and fear go hand in hand, you lose one, you can kiss goodbye to the other. I don't give a toss what anyone says. At base level, that's how human beings operate.' He finished his pint. 'Fancy another?'

'Yes, why not?' Frank said. 'Why not?'

Chapter 50

Ian Grant was sitting down in Interview Room Three. Opposite him sat Ray and Paul. The recording device was switched off and Ian had not requested a solicitor. Initially, Ray had told Ian that they were waiting for a senior officer and they had sat in silence for a few minutes. When Paul had then entered the room, Ian's head rocked back in a manner Ray recognised and he saw Ian raise his eyebrows for a moment.

In fact, Ray had already exonerated Ian, both by putting him on the official books as an informant and by gaining clearance from Frank that he could approach him for their last meeting. Nevertheless, Paul was now giving him a bit of a rough ride.

'What I want to know, is why you didn't tell us your people were armed?' Paul raised his voice. 'You got two men killed!'

'Nah, but I did tell you though,' Ian said, calmly.

'Erm, yes he did guv. I didn't get the text,' Ray interjected. Paul rounded on Ray, wondering if this was true or not. Ray took his phone from his pocket. 'Look,' he said.

Sure enough, Ian had sent a further text some time later. *"Come propa tooled up, is armed."* Paul read the text message and Ray thought he saw a flicker of a smile cross his face, but it swiftly vanished into a frown.

'Just as well for you, then, that you decided to help us out,' Paul said, scowling at Ian. 'Otherwise the Firearms Unit would have put your arse in a sling, boy.' Ian sat staring in front of him. He said nothing. 'Ray here, he tells me you're looking at joining us,' Paul continued, his expression unchanged.

Ian nodded. 'Yeah,' he said. Ray saw him gulp under Paul's long, hard stare.

'Good,' concluded Paul. There was a brief pause. 'You know there's a fitness test, don't you?' added Paul, suddenly grinning at Ian. 'Better getting running, fat arse.'

Ian grinned back. 'Yeah, well,' he said, 'make a change running for you, than the other way.'

Ray saw Paul smile broadly. The two men looked at one another. 'It's a better direction,' Paul replied, 'in the long run.' He looked at Ian, straight in the eyes and nodded at him a few times. 'Trust me,' said Paul. 'I know.'

* * *

It had been the Serious Organised Crime Association, SOCA, who had confirmed that the group they had arrested was part of a wider network; a Chinese gang, based in London. Simultaneously, whilst undertaking the raid in Tarnside, a separate SOCA squad had been busting down the door of a building in Chinatown, London. Another ten kilos of China White had been recovered from a cellar, the door of which had been locked by twin sliding bolts that ran across a steel door. A further five men had also been arrested, one of whom was considered to be a faction leader. It was a major bust, even by the standards of SOCA and the Metropolitan police force. As a result, it received a large amount of publicity.

In addition, the footprints that had been found at the murder scene of John Harrington were matched to Tony Parkes and the other two Chinese men that had been arrested in the Tarnside raid. The CCTV image, of the man that Jason had suspected, turned out to be an erroneous lead. The news was still all over the front page of the local newspaper when it dropped through the letterbox the following week.

Rosie Blake had spent the days following her release scouring aerial images of every island off the English coast until, finally, she had identified a garden that she recognised. High brick walls, a private beach, an elegant mansion; it was definitely the same place! Rosie was quite certain. Excitedly, she had immediately reported the location, a small island in the Bristol Channel, to the Detective Chief Superintendent, Albert Manson. She had then swiftly ascertained that the house was owned by an English gentlemen, a Mr. Jeffrey Steer. Tracking him down proved straightforward enough, but it transpired that he did not live there. The house was usually available for rent, as finding tenants was not easy; however, it had recently been leased by a foreign investment firm, Dragon Holdings, apparently based in the Far East. Further investigations revealed the transactions had been undertaken via a network of accounts and agents. Eventually, Rosie discovered that Dragon Holdings was no longer operational, having recently declared insolvency. Despite the company being registered in China, it appeared the former Trustees resided in Burma. Since independence from the United Kingdom was granted in 1948, Burma has endured ongoing, civil conflicts, now stretching back over sixty years. The country remains outside of Interpol and beyond the scope of normal international policing. In the light of recent, fresh uprisings propelling the nation into the grip of one of the bloodiest episodes to date, it quickly became apparent that there was absolutely no chance of co-operation with the British from the Burmese authorities.

***

Now the end of August, the summer sunshine had given England a rare, farewell blast over the Bank Holiday weekend. The country had baked, temperatures reaching thirty-two degrees Celsius in central London and exceeding thirty over much of the south. Sitting upon one of the green benches overlooking the beach on the Bank Holiday Monday afternoon, Ray wondered quite how so much could have changed for him, so quickly. After years of lonely monotony, he felt excited about the future for the first time in eons. Still slightly unsure of where the relationship may be heading, Ray had decided to commit to Ellie and hope for the best. He turned to look at her, as she sat, perched next to him and throwing bread high up into the air for the seagulls to catch on the wing. She caught him looking and smiled, pushing blonde hair back from her face. Throwing the last of the bread to the sky, she shuffled up along the bench and snuggled up to him, wrapping her hands around his arm and laying a head on his shoulder.

Ellie was quite sure about her choice of partner. She turned and kissed him on the cheek. 'You know,' she said, 'I have always wanted to go to France. On a holiday.'

'France!' Ray said. He turned and looked at her, aghast. 'You have got to be joking!'

THE END

DS Jackson will be back…

Further information on the next instalment of the DS Jackson series will be announced in <u>2015</u>

This is just the beginning.

It is not over.

Printed in Great Britain
by Amazon.co.uk, Ltd.,
Marston Gate.